DOCTOR WHO

BELTEMPEST

JIM MORTIMORE

Published by BBC Worldwide Ltd
Woodlands, 80 Wood Lane
London W12 0TT

First published 1998
Reprinted 1999

Copyright © Jim Mortimore 1998
The moral right of the author has been asserted

Original series broadcast on the BBC
Format © BBC 1963
Doctor Who and TARDIS are trademarks of the BBC

ISBN 0 563 40593 7
Imaging by Black Sheep, copyright © BBC 1998

Printed and bound in Great Britain by Mackays of Chatham
Cover printed by Belmont Press Ltd, Northampton

for
Steve
*'Because I draw on the temporal psychic energy
of all spankings through the ages'*
Cole

– definitely
one of the good guys

Prologue

Even stars die.

They may grow old, they may seem inconceivable when held against the flickering candle of our own existence, yet they too have lives that are shaped by the same universe, the same immutable laws as are our own lives.

In the measure of Deep Time the brief moment of existence of all the stars in the universe is as the moment a butterfly lives compared with all the summers that will ever be. For the red giant, galactic summer is over and winter is approaching. Its hydrogen fuel long since exhausted, this old, mad sun has consumed its inner worlds and barely noticed their absence. Burning helium now as a lingering precursor to death, the red giant prepares to shrug off its outer mantle of remaining hydrogen and take its remaining family of planets with it into oblivion.

Within the star, a schism: its core shrinking and growing ever hotter even as its outer layers expand and cool. Soon now will come the moment of death, of explosion – the surviving solar matter burning in a tiny incandescent lump at the heart of a nebula composed of the tattered shreds of its own corpse.

Still from death comes life. A truth unchanging while there is yet energy in the universe.

While the red giant continues slowly to die, life on its many worlds continues to grow and evolve.

It was an old world, one from which the fire had gone. A dark backwater, an eddy in the current of life, with no bright future or destiny, forgotten by any who might once have observed it or experienced it for however brief a moment.

Its chill plains and freezing mountains, its sparse black vegetation and cold-sculpted animal life were left to just one pair of eyes to study: a single mind to look up at the sky and wonder if it would kill those who lived beneath it today, or play with them a while longer before dismissing them from this life.

Skywatcher glanced at the iron-grey clouds that scraped the tops of the White Mountains and tried to work out how long it would be before the snow on the ground covered the tracks of the fast-moving herd of hornrunners. Skywatcher and his brother, Fastblade, had been tracking the herd for three days. It was his responsibility to make sure the sky would allow this kill. If Fastblade did not find the hornrunners' winter nest before the snow concealed it from view, then many would die from starvation in the coming months, and the hornrunners would emerge from their hibernation to a world cleansed by cold of all but the most isolated – probably cannibalistic – pockets of human life.

Skywatcher pulled his furs more tightly around his chapped face, his nose clogged with the greasy stink of animal fat smeared upon his skin to protect it from the biting cold. Fastblade had no such protection. Fastblade needed every sense clear and unclouded. Whereas this weather was, for Skywatcher, the fear and wonder of a cruel friend, the same weather for Fastblade was little more than a tool with which he focused his mind acutely on the task at hand. The tracking of the nest.

Two very different men, then, Skywatcher and Fastblade. Yet, though the sky affected them in different ways, it made them brothers, too. For without the sky to determine their actions they would surely be little more than mindless animals living easily from an endless bounty of summer food. Skywatcher had heard many of the village curse the sky, the space above, the endless night drawing close about their world. He had heard the prayers to a dying sun, swollen with cold crimson light, whose nearness brought little comfort beyond the beauty of dawn and sunset across the frost-laden plains. But, unlike his fellow men, Skywatcher was not afraid. Not of the sky. How could he be? The sky was his friend and loved him. The sky brought him life in the form of birds too cold to fly, of snow to make water, of berries and meat preserved in the frost from one season to the next. Skywatcher knew where life came from on this world. And he loved the sky in turn for making every day a challenge, for making every hour and every moment linked and full of meaning, like the crystal spokes of a single snowflake.

Fastblade thought it was all birdlime, of course.

Fastblade hated the cold. Hated having to hunt. He took no pleasure in experience. He seemed little able to observe and think, and make connections, and totally unable to wonder about anything beyond where the next meal would come from to fill his belly. It had been many seasons since the moment when Skywatcher first realised that the number of people who thought like Fastblade was increasing with every generation, whereas the number of people like himself was growing smaller. It was a moment that had shaped his life. But it was also one of which he had told nobody – for who would understand his view, or care?

In that moment of realisation, Skywatcher knew his people were dying. Not as individuals but as a species, unable to adapt to the conditions prevalent on their world, conditions that grew harsher every desiccated season. Sometimes he wondered what would follow after they had all died – whether there would simply be nothing at all, or whether some other form of life would take their place to hunt the hornrunners beneath an ever more swollen sun.

It was a question to which Skywatcher knew he would never have an answer. But that did not matter. For the question itself was simply one more experience, one more crystal spoke on the snowflake that was his world and his life.

Hunting food was, too – as Skywatcher was reminded when a young hornrunner erupted from an early nest a man's length from him and, defending that nest, charged him with all seven horns articulated into the position of attack.

Fastblade saw the movement of snow a heartbeat too late. Yelling a warning to Skywatcher, he launched himself across the snow, dagger drawn, teeth exposed in a furious scream.

Skywatcher was frozen in place before the animal bursting from the snow in front of him. Fool. Dreamer. If he died the tribe died with him. Did he not know this? Did he not care?

Wasting no time on recriminations, Fastblade lurched across packed snow, his furs a cumbersome demand on his reserves of energy, even while protecting him from the killing cold. Above, the iron-grey clouds were moving ever closer, bringing a murky crimson darkness with the promise of more snow. Closer, the hornrunner had now emerged from its burrow and was skimming the ground on six triple-jointed legs, the pads that served for feet slapping almost silently against the snow and sending swirls of white powder into the heavy air.

Quick as Fastblade was, his eyes were quicker. Even as he ran they were searching the tableau for an advantage. There was none.

The hornrunner reached Skywatcher, who now tried to hurl himself clear of the enraged animal. All seven horns had locked forward into the attack position. The hornrunner was a young animal, massing barely twice as much as Skywatcher – but still it would be enough to kill him should even one of those horns bite home into his body.

Skywatcher dived – and the hornrunner caught him with three horns while still in midair.

A moment later Fastblade leapt clumsily on to the animal's back and drove his dagger into the furred gap between the bony plates at the base of the animal's skull. The hornrunner reared and Fastblade found himself flying through the air. The ground punched the breath from his body. He looked up to find himself eye to compound eye with the hornrunner. It was dead of course. He knew that from the lustre of the many lenses in the eye, the coating of frost already forming there as the animal's body heat was leached away by the wind and the storm of snow its own death had thrown into the air.

Fastblade retrieved his dagger, cleaned it, then staggered to where Skywatcher lay moaning on the ground.

One of the runner's horns had snapped cleanly off and emerged from the bloodstained furs cladding Skywatcher's thigh. More blood leaked from wounds in his shoulder and arm. But the worst wound was in his chest. Blood pumped sluggishly, staining the furs there, showing no sign of abating.

Skywatcher blinked, his face pale even beneath the layer of animal fat. More blood flecked his lips. He tried to speak. No words came, just an animal-like moan of pain. His eyes closed and opened spasmodically.

Fastblade ripped open Skywatcher's furs and began to pack handfuls of freezing snow against the chest wound. Skywatcher groaned. Fastblade wasted no time on words. If Skywatcher died the tribe died with him. If he lived – well, there would be time enough for blame then. Otherwise –

Fastblade packed the snow as tight as he could against Skywatcher's chest. But even as he did this he knew the effort was useless. For every handful of fresh white snow he brought, the balance was stained pink by the release of Skywatcher's lifeblood.

A weak movement beside him stopped Fastblade's activities. Skywatcher's hand grasped feebly at the furs at his wrist. Fastblade batted the hand aside and continued with his work.

Then he looked into Skywatcher's eyes. They were gazing mutely at the sky from which he took his name.

Blood bubbled at chapped lips. Skywatcher was trying to speak. Fastblade leaned closer but Skywatcher's voice had no strength. Instead his finger managed to point upward.

Following his indication, Fastblade looked up. His mouth dropped open in mute astonishment.

Through a jagged break in the iron-grey clouds Fastblade could see the sky. And the sun, a swollen crimson globe partially obscured by three circles of darkness – a triple eclipse, impossible on a world that knew only one moon.

Cradling his brother in his arms, Fastblade gazed in stupefaction at the impossible sight and cried aloud. If he felt Skywatcher's life depart he did not know it.

The three dark circles conjoined, obscuring the swollen girth of the sun and plunging the world into unexpected darkness.

Fastblade had seen an eclipse before. He sank to the ground beside his dead brother, his eyes aching from the sudden lack of red light, and waited for the light to return.

When it finally reappeared the sun was dark, a seething black shell with occasional bursts of light from within.

Fastblade prayed for his brother as the night grew colder and darker. He waited for morning to bury Skywatcher, but morning did not come for more than a year.

* * *

Skywatcher planted the bone spade and tipped a last stack of snow across the grave. Fastblade had been the last hunter to die. Like the others he had died night-blind, raving in his sleep from fever and the visions. Now he joined them in endless sleep, their bodies preserved for ever by cold in a world that had known but a flicker of light for more than a year.

Skywatcher remembered the stories Fastblade had told him of his, Skywatcher's, father and how he had died because he was careless. Now Fastblade himself was dead. He, Skywatcher, was the eldest now – even though in Fastblade's eyes he had been little more than a child.

A child who had seen a sun die and a world end. Who had seen crops fail and people kill each other in their mad desire for food. A child, now a man, who waited only for death.

The last spadeful of snow hit the grave and Skywatcher patted it down. Then he looked up at the cloudless sky and at the stars – and the circular patch of darkness shot through with occasional threads of fire which marked the position of the dead sun. He wondered if his father would have known what this meant. The sky had changed with his father's death – as though the two events were linked. But were they, really? And did it matter? Skywatcher barely had the strength to lift the spade. There had been no food for half a season and most the tribe was dead.

Skywatcher put down the bone spade. He sat beside the grave. What should he do now? His mind, having been occupied by the work of digging, now returned to its long fear: that with no food there remained no choice but to wait for death.

Skywatcher felt madness take him then. He jumped up and began to dance, a clumsy lurching movement in the agonising cold. He began to sing, too – nonsense words, children's words. He felt like a child, felt on the verge of something he could not name, felt his heart sing in his chest, beating a rhythm to which his life kept time. A tiny part of his mind wondered what would happen when his heart lost the beat – whether he would notice the end of the song. Whether he would notice his own death. Then the song took him again and he lost himself in the madness.

So it was that he missed the miracle: others witnessed it and later told him of it, but Skywatcher, in his madness, missed the moment for which he had taken his name. The moment in which light and life returned to his world, with a new, impossible sun.

The old red giant is gone, in its place a younger, warmer star.

A momentary flush of life on the innermost planet is replaced by another threat of extinction, this time not from cold but from heat.

Centuries pass. Aeons. Throughout the solar system other changes are taking place. Old life, dying among the outer planets, is given another lease by the heat and light of this newer, more temperate star. New life on the innermost world is placed under threat. The evolutionary imperative for survival throughout the changing solar system is renewed.

While the yellow main-sequence star itself progresses slowly through a second impossible infancy, life on its many worlds continues to grow and evolve.

It is a process observed fleetingly by three planet-sized masses as their orbits carry them beyond a solar system now flourishing with the new life they have inadvertently made possible.

Part One

Chapter One

There is only one truth and that truth is endless and that truth is death.

Eldred Saketh rehearsed his final speech in his head, bringing the 'corder close by to ensure it caught every passionately enunciated word and pious expression as he stepped out on to the lava field to die.

His face was calm despite the torturous heat rising from the molten rock amid clouds of toxic steam. His farewells and preparations were said, his life was now surrendered gladly so that he might enter his Endless State.

Saketh knew he had only moments to live. He had no regrets. If his life had taught him anything it was that life itself was simply a muddled and inaccurate definition of that which was not Endless – a state of emotional frenzy with no clear focus or objectives, a state that did little more than dilute the truth and purity of the Endless State of Unbeing which was death.

Truth and purity were best for people. The thousands who had preceded him on to the surface of Belannia II had understood that. Yet still there were millions – billions – who did not understand. Their lives were small, insignificant points of no dimension, circumscribed by their hollow loves and self-serving desires. They did not understand the truth. Life was fear. Life was confusion. Life was helplessness. Life was pain.

The Endless was the removal of such pain. Those who were Endless now understood that. So too would the billions to come once they had experienced at second hand the glorious inception of his Endless State.

Of course you couldn't put it quite like that. You had to tell the truth in terms they could understand. You had to quote scriptures and mention rewards and eternal life after death. It was a process Eldred had found over the years to be both rewarding and frustrating in equal measures: a perfect balance – and a perfect illustration of the unnecessary and impure complexity of anything not Endless.

Now, in recognising his frustration and anger at the need to obscure the truth with pretty lies in order to give people the greatest gift of all for free, Eldred also recognised his own weakness, his own fallacy, his own state of impure complexity. It was time to purify himself and therefore his message.

The Message.

Eldred carefully rehearsed his final words again. They were the most important words he would ever speak. The future of his belief depended upon them. The speech was beautiful in its simplicity. It could not possibly fail to be understood by anyone who heard it.

Seeing no reason to wait any longer, Eldred began to speak. He spoke the words slowly, with gravity befitting their importance, rejoicing in the near-intolerable pain the toxic air brought to his throat and lungs in exchange for their utterance.

Then, screaming in what he told himself was exultation, Eldred Saketh fell convulsing upon the very edge of the lava field and waited impatiently to die.

And waited. And burned. And screamed. And *waited*. But he did not die. Instead he found a new Message. This new Message even had a Sign.

Above Eldred Saketh's frenziedly thrashing body, above the lava fields and the toxic air of Belannia II, the ferocious yellow ball of incandescent hydrogen, which for thousands of aeons had provided life and stability in a system already old beyond its time, began once more to change.

Eyes closed, elegant fingers loosely clasping copies of both *Hospital Station* by James White and *Green Eggs and Ham* by Dr Seuss, which he had been reading simultaneously, the Doctor stretched out one leg from his sand-locked, palm-shaded deck chair and nudged the replay button he'd recently wired into the Ship's gramophone with the toe of his left shoe.

The stretch was a bit of an effort, but not as much of an effort as moving the chair closer to the music system – also sand-locked a little further up the beach from the sun-brightened waves – would have been.

At his touch, the button – a bright, red, palm-sized emergency shutdown control removed from the drive generator of a junked sandminer – sank home with a satisfying clunk and, after the appropriate attendant clashing of gears and slippage of gramophone needles across sandy wax, the music system obligingly began to warble a repeat of Louis Armstrong's 'We Have All The Time In The World'.

The Doctor sighed happily.

Exactly 6,000,000,215 nanoseconds and one line of poignantly enunciated lyric later, a woman's voice said quietly from the sand beside him, 'Wouldn't it be easier just to put ten copies of the record on to the spindle?'

The Doctor stretched luxuriously. 'You know what I like most about you, Sam?' he said, then immediately answered his own rhetorical question: 'The way you ask such challenging questions.'

Samantha Jones frowned. In the same quite, adult tone of voice, she said, 'Thank you, Doctor. And I really like the way you still think of me as a child.'

The Doctor leapt to his feet. The motion was effortless, the speed dizzying. He bounced lightly on his toes for a moment, relishing the feel of gravity fighting with his own inertia. 'My dear Sam, the aquatic Crocodilians of Aquaatus VI are subjected to such terrible physical trauma from their environment that their intelligent, telepathic embryos are born so brain-damaged their only useful function is as a protective host for another intelligent, telepathic embryo.'

'That,' Sam said, 'is utterly distasteful.'

'The point being: childhood is relative.' The Doctor considered, then added rapidly, 'Except, of course, when the child in question is also a relative, in which case the relativity becomes relative and, er, well, you do see where we're going with this, don't you?'

Sam affected nonchalance. 'No. But wherever it is we're making good time.'

The Doctor casually studied the relative levels of quartz and fossilised animal matter present in fifty-three of the closest grains of sand. 'Relatively speaking, Sam, nothing is going nowhere. And, given the current energy state of the universe, nothing is definitely going nowhere with a relative speed greater than the most excited subatomic particle.' The Doctor stopped bouncing and instead began to pace. He did this with the same manic intensity with which he did everything, including thinking. The fifty-three grains of sand – along with several thousand others – were displaced by his feet as easily as they were displaced by his mind.

Sam sighed. 'Manifestly,' she said with all the patience she could muster.

The Doctor stopped pacing suddenly. 'I don't suppose you're old enough to have offspring yet, are you?'

'Children, you mean?' Sam blew out her cheeks and huffed

mightily. 'Now *there's* a conversational leap of biblical proportions.'

The Doctor waited.

Sam said, 'I love you when you're in a rhetorical mood. Kids. Well. Yeah. Sure I want them. Doesn't everyone? Don't you?'

The Doctor opened his mouth to respond but Sam was already continuing, 'Don't worry. The question's rhetorical. The idea of all that pain bringing forth new life is horrible but – you know – kind of interesting. I mean, why does it have to hurt like that? I mean – it's hardly pro-evolution, is it? If women were sensible they'd all have babies in test tubes and nobody would need to be hurt again, right?'

The Doctor frowned. 'Tell that to the test tube.'

Sam giggled. 'You what?'

'Just my morbid little joke. Forget it.'

Sam frowned. 'Whatever. Anyway… what about you? Do you have a family?'

'We talked about this before, Sam. Don't you remember?'

'That was then. I've got a new perspective now.'

The Doctor smiled. 'I like to think of the universe itself as my foster family. It took me in when I was young. Taught me about life when my own parents decided to opt out of their responsibilities. It was kind to me when I needed it and so I look after it from time to time – keep it hanging together, you might say, through its old age…'

Sam laughed. 'That's a metaphor, right?'

'Is it?' The Doctor did not smile. 'You never met my parents, did you?'

Sam shivered suddenly. Time to change the subject. 'Do you know *everything*?'

Now the Doctor did smile, and his face lit up with mischievous delight. 'My dear Sam, we live in an age of information supersaturation. Even I cannot know everything. An incarnation of mine once said, "Sometimes you've got to be dim to be brilliant".'

'That,' said Sam, 'is an oxymoron.'

'But of course,' chirped the Doctor merrily. 'What's the point of being an oxygen breather if you can't be a moron?'

Sam's frown deepened disapprovingly. 'And that's a pun.'

'Is it? Oh dear.' The Doctor's face assumed an expression of such gravity he felt it might collapse under its own weight. 'Perhaps we should continue this conversation over breakfast.'

Sam allowed herself the faintest smile. 'Green eggs and ham?' She nodded at the Doctor's first choice of leisure-time reading. 'Not very vegetarian. I think I'll pass.'

The Doctor glanced at the book as well; the smile remained but went a little odd around the corners.

Sam added, 'But I might just have some toast. If we can have it here on the beach.'

The Doctor frowned, glanced quickly around himself, then blinked – apparently in amazement. 'Yes, yes, of course, you're quite right, quite right! A beach! Obvious, really. You know,' he added to Sam in tones of childlike delight, 'I never thought of it like that before. As silicon, yes, mica, quartz in powder form, various geological formations concealing numerous species of biological life assaulted continuously by liquid in a high-energy state.' He sat cross-legged at the edge of the surf and crumbled a handful of sand between his fingers. 'But never as a *beach*.' He glanced pointedly at Sam and rushed on excitedly: 'Sometimes you can get so caught up in the brushstrokes you fail to see the whole picture.'

Sam thought for a moment about the time she had spent away

from the TARDIS, the things she'd learnt about herself – the things she thought she'd learned. 'Are you trying to tell me something?'

The Doctor grinned with all the crooked charm of a child thief. 'Only that I like my eggs sunny side up and my ham green.'

Sam felt a smile sneak across her lips. 'You're impossible,' she said with a smile.

The Doctor smiled back. 'Manifestly,' he said.

And that was when the beach exploded.

'What's going on!' Sam spat the words out with a mouthful of sand as she felt herself lifted and slammed against the heaving beach. A short distance away the previously tranquil waves were spiralling up into an ice-green mountain of water. It looked very, very hard. She screwed her eyes shut, then immediately opened them. She was *not* going to die with her eyes shut, that was for sure.

Some distance away the Doctor was standing with both feet planted squarely on the heaving beach, trying to rescue his records from the gramophone. His voice came as a distant sigh upon the howl of displaced air. 'Something I hadn't anticipated. Some kind of gravitational disturbance.' Seventy-eights sprayed into the air as the Doctor was rocked by another heavy disturbance. Waves lapped around his feet. Sparks erupted from the gramophone. 'Yes, yes, I know, the old thing seems to be having a bit of a problem with it. Unusual to say the least, yes, very unusual – not to mention a tad worrying.'

'You can forget the excuses!' Sam howled above the noise of splitting rock. 'If you didn't want breakfast all you had to do was say!' She ducked as a palm tree sailed overhead to smash against the airborne shoreline. A rain of coconuts followed. 'Now will you please just sort it out before we're both killed!'

'Going to try ejecting bits of the architecture to stabilise the –'
The rest of the Doctor's reply was lost to Sam. Sand that had been
whipped into airborne dunes by the wind dumped itself in
choking tons over her and everything went dark.

It wasn't dark for very long. Just long enough for her to get very
scared and short of breath. Then the shaking began again,
together with a terrible screaming sound – a noise like planets
being torn apart by the errant child of some hideous god.

The sound increased, and the shaking, and so did the pain in her
chest as she tried really hard to hold out for air to breathe instead
of sand.

She felt a pressure behind her eyes matching the pressure of
sand on them, opened her mouth to scream, swallowed sand, then
found herself falling, rolling, gasping for air and choking up the
sand she had swallowed.

She opened her eyes. She was in a park. The ground was shaking.
The sky was a glass dome through which the beautiful green-grey
bulk of an ocean world loomed. Lights from cities blotched the
surface of the planet. The lights were moving, floating. Stars shone,
hard points, beyond the planet. There was wind. Lots of it. The
small sand dune she was floundering in was whipped away from
her in abrasive streamers that scraped at her arms and face.

A palm tree, presumably uprooted from the TARDIS beach, fell
close by and Sam rolled away quickly.

The scream of rending metal had become the scream of air
emptying through a crack in the sky. And the scream of people
trying to leave the enclosed park area.

People. Lots of people. Lots of *panicking* people.

Where was the TARDIS? How had she got off? Where was she
now?

She struggled to her feet, aware the air was thinning, that the last particles of sand were being dragged by the air currents along with every leaf, every bit of dirt and a number of small, screeching animals, towards the widening crack in the sky.

She ran across the shaking ground, swept up in the crowd, dragged by it as first bushes and then small, ornamental trees swept up towards the looming planet.

She felt hands curled into desperate fists pummelling her; she fell, curled away from uncaring feet; she saw a wall of green-painted metal loom before her, wide hatches gliding shut, halting as the ground twisted violently, then buckling, to jam half open as people poured through them, as a familiar sound called her to turn, to see the TARDIS appear in the middle distance in a flood of sand and water, to tip, to fall into the chasm opening across the section of woodland, to vanish from sight as she was dragged screaming from the park.

She wasn't the only one screaming. Everyone – *everything* – else was screaming, too. The people fleeing the garden, the atmosphere forcing itself through the jammed airlock; even the ground was screaming as the foundations buckled and the sky tore and the city began to empty itself into vacuum.

She felt herself being pulled backwards by the slipstream and pushed in as many different directions as there were people around her. Occasionally a voice rose above the gestalt scream of the dying city.

'– spaceport, get to the –'

'– here, Jenny, come here! Stay with me or you'll –'

'– it's coming down, the roof's –'

'– are you? Jenny, where –'

Sam felt herself carried along helplessly in this tidal wave of people, swept along in an endless moment of fear and panic. She felt hands grabbing at her, pushing, tugging at her clothes and hair; she felt nails rake across her cheek as the scream of the city tore at her ears, got into her head, sandblasted her mind with what seemed to be every fearful moment she'd ever experienced.

Then it stopped. Or, rather, no. It didn't stop: *she* stopped. She stopped being *scared*.

The screaming continued, but it was just sound now, just the sound of other people's fear. With this knowledge to arm herself against the surprise at her sudden lack of fear, Sam found she was able to stand fast against the crowd, moving sideways, dodging fists, ignoring blows she could not avoid, until she reached the side of the corridor, where she pressed herself against a wide pane of glass with the words

BLACK ROCK MINING
Equipment – Supplies – Claims Registered
Quality Work – Lifetime Guarantee

written on it.

Sam watched the crowd rush past, felt the air thin around her, then turned away to face the glass. She had to think. The Doctor was gone. The TARDIS was gone. Five minutes from now the air would also be gone. Shortly after that her life would be gone. The glass of the shopfront seemed to ripple like water with the reflections of the people streaming past. Her own reflection seemed to gaze right back out of the shop at her, eyes wide, cheek furrowed by parallel scratches and streaked with her own blood. *Think,* she told herself. You're an adult. Adults don't panic, they don't scream, they don't run. They don't trample each other, they don't lose their kids, they don't suffocate or get crushed, or –

– die. They don't *die* they don't –

They were going to die.

She was going to die.

Sam leaned her face against the glass, tried not to imagine what her body would look like emptied of life, bloated and burst from decompression; tried not to imagine how much it would hurt, how much it was *already* hurting.

She pressed her face harder against the glass, hoping the pain from her cheek would let her focus on the problem, and find a solution to it. Nothing. Just the glass. The reflections. The shop, with shelves of equipment racked ready for sale or use.

She grinned. The movement caught her cheek by surprise; it took a moment for the muscles to catch up with her thoughts, and then when they did, the pain was very, very bad.

But the smile persisted.

She knew what she had to do.

She picked up a chunk of fallen synthocrete, hefted it and hurled it as hard as she could against the glass, which cracked, ever so slightly. A few more blows had the window lying in smashed ruins, the debris already peeling away in a jagged rain. Sam stepped over the sill and began to rummage among the equipment. They had to be here. They just had to. What self-respecting purveyor of quality mining supplies did not carry –

– *oxygen supplies!*

And here they were.

Gratefully cracking open a cylinder and breathing from the mask, Sam wondered what to do next. The stream of people outside had slowed but not stopped.

In fact some of them had paused in their flight long enough to look in through the smashed window. Some of them had even thought, as Sam had done, what might be found there.

Now several were clambering over the sill into the shop.

'It's OK,' Sam mumbled through her mask. 'There's plenty of air. Look. It's over here. Just grab a cylinder and –'

The people ignored her.

The people grabbed the cylinders of air.

The people ripped the mask from her face.

The people then attacked each other in order to keep the most air for themselves.

All the while the pressure fell.

Sam gasped, knocked sideways by an uncaring fist, sprawled among the knocked-over shelves of equipment.

She tried to find the strength to crawl away from the mob before being trampled in the search for more supplies. There was no strength left. All her energy was used up simply sucking air from the depleted atmosphere.

Her head spun.

Lights flickered before her eyes.

Where was the Doctor?

A figure moved over her. She tried to cower but could not move. A face swam closer, and Sam saw it was wearing an oxygen mask. The Doctor? No. The apparent age was right but the hair was too short, and the face too gaunt, the expression too… immediate. Too right here and now. And the Doctor did not wear a cowl or habit.

'Help.' The word came out with a gasp, a tiny exhalation of the last breath she had.

The priest glanced at her and his face twisted with real compassion. He nodded. Sam shuddered with relief. Saved. She waited for air. Air did not come. The priest did not remove his oxygen mask.

She tried to gasp out a plea for help. She had no breath to deliver it. Her skin was prickling as the pressure continued to fall.

Help me! Please!

The priest offered a dazzling smile from behind the mask. 'There is only one truth.' His voice barely rose above the sound of escaping atmosphere. 'And that truth is endless, and that truth is death.'

Surgeon Major Alesis Conaway swore as the steel door finally rolled up into the ceiling of the corridor and the airflow suddenly increased. The upper body of the man she had been treating for a broken arm was no longer attached to its legs.

'Sealant, give me some sealant. And a cauteriser. And blood. Two litres, Unidonor, and –' she stopped. The man – dressed in the cold blue of Administration – was clearly beyond help. She swore again. His eyes were still open. She wondered if she had been the last thing they'd seen.

She stood up. 'The hydroponicum's that way, half a click.' She pointed through the hatch. 'You, you, you, you and you – get it sorted. You and you, clear the body. And I don't want to hear any arguments about who gets the messy bit.'

You, you, you, you and you were halfway through the hatch when their passage was collectively blocked by an average-sized man of medium build and large presence, who was bouncing agitatedly from one foot the other while simultaneously adjusting his cravat, brushing at a rather crumpled frock coat and shaking sand from a thick mop of unruly hair.

'You,' he said, pointing at the nearest nurse. 'And you, and you, and you and you, come with me right away. We have to help the old girl. We have to get her out. We have to do it now, or –'

Conaway barged through the skirmish line of nurses. This was all she needed: a panicking citizen making her job harder than it already was. 'Shut up. If you can walk, then walk that way to the spaceport, only don't walk – run. Otherwise, I'll assume you're panicking and sedate you. Then of course, I'd have the whole sorry business of informing your next of kin when we didn't have time to get you aboard a ship.'

The man bounced up and down on his toes. He seemed agitated. Or excited. Or frightened. Or possibly just mad. 'No.' He waved his hands – 'wrung' might have been a better word. 'No no no no no, you don't understand, you really don't understand. It's very simple, really. You see, she's saved my life on more than one occasion, quite a lot more than one occasion actually, and so I really don't feel justified in leaving her to –'

Conaway sighed. She turned to a nurse. 'Jab him. ten cc's benzoprophyliticine.' To the man she added, 'In case you hadn't noticed, I've got some people to save.'

The nurse was a professional. He moved very fast, but as fast as he was, the strange man was faster. In the time it took the nurse to unholster his tranquilliser gun the man had removed his frock coat, rolled up his left sleeve, crouched to remove a shoelace, stood up again, tied it single-handedly around his arm just above his elbow, extended the arm towards the nurse and was busy tapping his forearm to bring up a vein.

As Conaway watched, the man stared straight at her. He was absolutely motionless now except for the fingers of his right hand tapping on his left arm. Tap, tuh-tap, tuh-tap-tap, tap-tuh-tap. She became aware that the fingers were beating out a rather impatient freeform jazz rhythm.

The nurse was used to treating people like this. He didn't wait for instructions. He simply availed himself of the proffered arm and administered a slightly larger dose of tranquilliser than Conaway had ordered.

Nothing happened.

After a few seconds, nothing continued to happen.

Then the rather eccentric man undid the shoelace, rolled down his sleeve, retrieved a cufflink from his shirt pocket, breathed on it, polished it, fastened his sleeve with it, put his coat back on and twirled the shoelace absently in front of his body like an old-fashioned biplane with one damaged engine. 'In case *you* hadn't noticed, I've got a *planet* to save.' The strange man turned and began to run down the corridor, in the direction of the airflow, one shoe flapping distractedly as he did so.

'By the way,' he called back over his shoulder, while kicking free the flapping shoe. 'I'm the Doctor. And you are…?'

'Surgeon Major Alesis Conaway.' The words seemed to come out automatically.

'Excellent,' called the Doctor, somehow managing to inject a smile into his voice from a distance of fifty metres. He turned to face her. 'Glad to be working with you. Now, I know this is going to seem a little peremptory, not to mention somewhat outside the chain of command, but, under the circumstances, I would suggest that quick thought and independent action are more than justified if we are to save lives.'

'Which is what I am trying to do.'

'Yes, quite, quite. I am sure that you are in your own small way, although perhaps we could get into the business of self-congratulation at a more appropriate time. You see, if I am correct, your presence here is merely a stopgap, someone to alleviate the symptoms; very laudable, of course – lives are always worth saving, no matter what the general population trends and how you might be increasing the severity of any hypothetical ultimate Malthusian control which might be lurking in the wings by using technology to avert a more immediate natural disaster – but nonetheless you really should be applying yourselves to the cause of the problem and solving that, even if it happens to be at the cost of more immediate lives, D'you see? Of course, that's the textbook theory. My own take is somewhat more humanitarian. I say, save everyone now and worry about the consequences later. D'you agree?'

Conaway wondered how much medication this man who called himself a Doctor was already on. 'This moon is undergoing tectonic stress,' she told him. 'Nobody knows the reason. The entire *city* is collapsing. That's twenty-three million people, in case you hadn't noticed.'

'I'm glad to see you've finally cut through to the nub of the problem. And, if you can just help me reach the old girl, there's a rather wonderful thing inside called a gravitic stabiliser which I can use to generate a zone of tectonic stability around the immediate area, if not the entire moon, assuming a planetary mass of roughly average proportions, of course, and I see no reason why we shouldn't do that. I mean, how often have you run across a solar body of anything less than average mass? Exactly,' he added without waiting for an answer. 'Very conservative thing, the average planetary body. Something to do with having such a wonderfully large moment of inertia, I shouldn't wonder. Ah, here we are, the hydroponicum. The old girl's in that large fissure.'

Conaway glanced up at the shattered sky and the last shreds of vaporous atmosphere being sucked out into the void. The stars were very bright. The grey-green hemisphere of Belannia VI was very beautiful. Conaway looked down at the ground. It was split in a wide crack. There seemed no bottom to the chasm. As she watched, a tree, its leaves stripped and its bark desiccated by the near-vacuum, toppled into the crack.

'Your friend's down there?'

'Yes, so you see there's no time to waste if we're to –'

'Then she's dead.'

'Ah, no,' the Doctor grinned sheepishly. 'You see it's a matter of… Did I mention that she isn't human?'

'Not human?'

'No.'

'Then what is she?'

'More a kind of blue box.'

Conaway blinked. 'A –'

'– box, yes. Blue. Simulated wooden exterior, yes; bit battered but did look rather smart once, so I've assured myself. Of course, that was a much older me and somewhat less reliable, not to mention more biased towards the design, I shouldn't wonder, though I grant you there are a great many aesthetic considerations to be said for an antique-exterior dimensional map, not the least of which is that I'd have thought she'd be pretty hard to miss among all that boring grey rock. So,' he added without actually stopping in the first place, 'if you could see your way clear to arranging for a couple of fathoms of rope I'll just –'

The shoelace, which the Doctor had been spinning continuously, suddenly fell slack in his hand. Then the hand fell limp beside his body. A glazed, somewhat distant look spread across his face, as if his mind had suddenly found somewhere much less interesting to be, which it had. Then, under the delayed influence of Conaway's tranquilliser, he fell over and began to snore.

The snoring, like the finger-tapping before it, also took the form of a rather impatient, freeform jazz rhythm.

The city died.

Five hundred years it had lived, generations it had seen born, and live, and die. It remembered all of them. Every name, every birth weight, every height; it remembered the colour of eyes, the shape of faces, every cubic centimetre of air and water and food consumed. It remembered every job performed, the use to which every hour of every person's leisure time was put. It remembered work. It remembered art. It remembered everything.

Though it was not alive, had no conscious awareness of itself as a living entity, nonetheless it was one. Though it did not generate a single spontaneous human thought, still it made decisions and cared for the people who lived within it. And, as a person was composed of the sum total of his memories, so too was the city composed of the sum total of its inhabitants. When the people died so it died with them. The catastrophic physical destruction that followed, the destruction of the moon on which it had been built, was merely inevitable detail.

The Doctor awoke once, much later, jammed in the hold of a medical frigate with several thousand refugees. His last woozy sight before lapsing once more into unconsciousness was of the moon beginning to break up and shower down into the atmosphere of Belannia VI in flaming chunks – one or two as big as small countries. His last thoughts as his eyes closed and greedy sleep claimed him again were not of the TARDIS – it was after all, indestructible – but of Sam, who was not.

Chapter Two

The first piece of debris struck the medical frigate while Conaway was preparing to amputate a crushed forearm. The patient was a nurse who'd been caught beneath a collapsed building, one of a team trying to free a number of refugees trapped there. The arm was as good as gone already but care had to be taken to ensure removal of the limb was conducted in such a way as to preserve as much nerve and muscle tissue as was possible in the event that a replacement limb, grown from the nurse's filed DNA, could be attached later.

That was the theory anyway. Practice was somewhat different – especially when there were large chunks of smashed-up moon colliding with the ship in whose medical bays you were operating.

'Atropine. Adrenaline. Anaesthesia: benzoprophyliticine, ten units per unit body mass. Berlioz: *Symphonie Fantastique*, first movement. Bonesaw.'

The theatre shook to a dull reverberating clang as another chunk of moon scraped an inordinately large section of paint from the hull. The lights flickered. The power supply to the bonesaw kicked over to its emergency generator. The lights came back up to full strength but the 'Reveries and Passions' of Hector Berlioz were abruptly struck dumb. The music was not on the emergency power circuit.

Conaway glanced irritably at the player and scowled. 'Never rains but it pours.' She picked up the saw.

The reverberating clang that had so annoyingly caused the abrupt cessation of the *Symphonie Fantastique* in the ship's operating theatre had a much more dramatic effect in the ship's main hold, where the Doctor was sitting up and looking somewhat distractedly around himself. The expression on his face suggested to one or two of the nearer refugees that he might have misplaced something. An item of luggage or a small child. The expression did not change, except that he became ever so slightly more interested as the reverberating clang developed quite suddenly into the hysterical screech of depressurisation.

'Clothes. Give me your clothes. All of them. Yes, right now. I know it's embarrassing but believe me the alternative is just a bit more than slightly less pleasant.' Without waiting for any replies, the Doctor dived into the nearest group of refugees, grabbing clothing at every turn until, like an ant rolling a seed the size of a bowling ball back to its nest, he heaved a large mass of clothing towards the nearest of the half-dozen jagged holes that had appeared in the hold.

The huge ball of clothing wedged itself tightly into the gap. The scream of rushing air abated momentarily. The Doctor added, 'Come along, don't be shy. Just imagine you're on Brighton beach and it's midsummer – there's another five holes to plug yet.'

Under the Doctor's coaxing and the moan of depressurisation alarms, the refugees began to strip.

When a maintenance crew appeared moments later wearing cheerful green spacesuits and carrying bright yellow canisters of foam sealant, they walked straight into the middle of a rugby scrum of half-naked people.

The technicians pulled off their space helmets and looked round in bemusement. One scratched his head. The Doctor took both of the large yellow canisters of foam and, one in each hand, began to seal the holes properly. He sang lustily as he worked.

'"There was I. Digging this hole. Hole in the ground. Big and sorta round it was…"'

Ten minutes later he returned the empty canisters to the technicians. The technicians glanced narrowly at the Doctor's fair skin and odd clothes.

' "The hole's not there. The ground's all flat. Underneath is the fellow with the bowler hat. And that's that." You know, Lorraine, I'm sure I've seen this before…' He added in a passably good Richard Dreyfuss impression, using clawed fingers to sculpt four roughly parallel lines down the side of his mountainous foam creation as it quickly set. Abruptly he snapped his attention back to the green-suited figures. 'That's right, I'm an alien.' He swept one arm in a grand gesture that encompassed both the seminaked refugees and the small hill of sodden material that was their clothing. 'Take me,' he added to the technicians with a faintly disturbing smile, 'to your laundry.'

There was a disconcertingly loud bang, immediately followed by a great number of smaller bangs and several scraping noises. More debris hitting the ship. Some of the refugees milled agitatedly. Somewhere a child began to cry.

'On second thoughts, perhaps you'd better just take me to your leader,' added the Doctor, more traditionally.

Captain Ruthelle Bellis gripped the deck rail of the bridge with one hand and a small photograph of her son and three-year-old grandson with the other, and asked the universe politely if it would stop throwing large rocks at her. All things considered, she felt she was too old for this sort of thing.

The universe clearly didn't agree with her.

The ship gonged and clanged on all sides, shaking to the sound of almost constant collisions, a sound that reached even here, the

31

inertia-dampened, gyro-mounted bridge. The nervesphere of the ship completely enclosed the Captain's podium. Her position was located at its heart, surrounded on all sides by systems operators, all of them strapped tightly into their workstations, some of them muttering to themselves as people are wont to do when trying to coax impossible responses from stubborn machinery, and at least one praying. Ranged in a wide arc in front of her were a number of three-dimensional displays showing the exterior of the medical frigate and surrounding space. The view panned and tracked in synch with her eyes as she looked left and right, up and down; everywhere she looked was rock. Smashed-up rock. Powdered rock. Gravel. Jagged chunks as large as mountains. Shattered plates which she guessed might be as big as small countries. Beyond the rock the grey-green hemisphere of Belannia VI was obscured by the glare of sunlight scattered through the cloud of fragments of pulverised moon. It was like a dazzling mist floating in space.

Bellis glanced around. She didn't need to hear the reports from the systems operators to know what the situation was. NerveNet was useless. Main power to the engines was fluctuating wildly – one engine cowling was mangled – and there was a jagged hole five hundred metres long where the dorsal sensor array had previously been located.

She gripped the picture of her family more tightly, crushing the coated photograph against the deck rail, as if trying to impress the features of her son and grandson on to the skin of her hand. From the left and above the captain's podium, a jagged chunk of rock cruised sullenly towards her. Despite a lifetime's experience, it was hard to resist the impulse to duck. 'Asteroid defences,' she snapped. 'Quick as you like, Mr Ranald.'

The gunnery officer did not turn. 'Tracking systems are still non-op, ma'am.'

I really didn't need to hear that.

'That last hit took out the secondary feeds from the back-up array.'

I really didn't need to hear that, either.

'Options?' Nobody spoke. 'If anyone's got any wild thoughts regarding last-minute salvation, now's the time to air them.'

No one spoke.

The rock spun lazily closer. Bellis gripped the deck rail even more tightly. She was looking at her death. The death of everyone aboard the ship.

'Update!' It was a desperate demand; she didn't need to hear the strained reply to know the truth.

'No change.'

She saw other pieces of debris impacting against the surface of the larger rock. The viewing systems were pulling in a crystal-clear image which, bearing in mind the beating the ship was taking, would've had their designers turning happy cartwheels. A hi-fidelity digital image of her own death, the shatter of rock, the bright glare of discharged energy following collision. The rock sparkled as it moved towards her – a sun-bright death-glare, rippling with light as it moved unstoppably closer.

She tore her eyes from the sight long enough to look at the photograph of her family. The paper was crushed, a broken crease slashed across the surface between the faces. She murmured their names. It was a prayer against the night, the muttered joy and curse of all ship's crew in the face of disaster. She tucked the crumpled paper back into her shirt pocket and looked up at the savage, whirling wall of rock. Inside she was screaming. Something in her ship had died and something in her head had died with it. She lifted a hand, fingers clenched into a fist, opened the fist palm outward as if to ward off the inevitable. The gesture was almost ludicrously futile. The rock just got bigger.

The podium elevator rose into place beside her. She barely managed to tear her eyes from the mesmerising sight of death bearing down upon her. The doors opened. Inside the elevator were two maintenance technicians and another man dressed in a long coat wearing only one shoe. The man bounced out of the elevator. 'Pleased to meet you,' he said. 'Captain Bellis, I presume,' he said. He looked up at the approaching rock, which now appeared to fill more than half of the available field of view, and his eyes opened very, very wide. He blinked.

'Ah,' he said, and began to rummage frantically in his pockets.

Surgeon Major Conaway lifted away the detached limb, bagged it for later gene harvesting, and turned her attention back to the truncated arm. She closed the major artery, sealed all the smaller veins and capped the exposed, shortened humerus. She removed pockets of fatty tissue from the flesh surrounding the bone, folded the prepared flaps of skin together across the end of the arm and began to weld.

She operated quickly, her movements owing more to desperation than precision, dictated by the sound of rocks crashing against the ship's hull which replaced the Berlioz she would normally be listening to. She'd been awake now for about thirty hours, only the last ten of which had been spent working in the capital city of Belannia VI's moon. She pinched the bridge of her nose tiredly, noticing only after a second or two that the nearest nurse had taken the skin-welder from her hand before she could accidentally stab herself in the eye with the hot end. She nodded her thanks and felt a momentary dizziness. She blinked. She felt cold. She could feel a slight wobble in her left knee, indication of muscle fatigue – a sure sign that she needed to rest.

Well, that was the theory, anyway.

'Speed?' The nurse noticed her tiredness, extracted a capsule from a small tin and offered it helpfully.

'And then some.' Conaway took the capsule and swallowed it. A moment later the operating theatre clicked sharply back into focus. Her knee stopped trembling. Her heart hammered for a moment and the settled to a steady rhythm. She sighed, picked up fresh skin-welder and checked the focusing lens.

On the bridge Captain Bellis felt like a spectator at a zero-g tennis match. After introducing himself and gazing with some interest at the approaching chunk of rock the Doctor had leapt off the captain's podium and, brandishing a number of objects grabbed from his pockets like a caveman brandishing several bone clubs, was now leaping effortlessly in the zero-gravity from station to station across the nervesphere.

At each terminal he would beam delightedly at the console operator, remove the hatch covering the interior of the console and stick his head and shoulders into the workspace thus revealed. He did this so fast and so consistently that soon a tangle of components and wires began to accumulate in the drift space between the consoles. Bits of circuit board – and indeed the Doctor himself from time to time – occasionally shot through the projected three-dimensional image of the rock with which they were still on an apparently irreversible collision course.

At the console on which he was working, one of the Doctor's arms – shirtsleeve rolled up like that of a mechanic or cricketer – emerged briefly, just long enough to thrust a confusing tangle of tools, electrical components and assorted chocolates at the bemused technician, who only then realised that the Doctor was handing him the contents of his pockets and not the contents of the computer on which he was working.

'Don't suppose you'd mind just holding these for me for a moment, would you, there's a good fellow.' The Doctor's voice emerged metallically from inside the console. 'They're getting in the way, and I've a bit of a tricky patient here. Have to reassure it everything's going to be OK before we start amputating.'

From the captain's podium Bellis watched as the rock grew bigger still.

The Doctor stuck his hand out of the console clicked his fingers. 'Screwdriver,' he snapped. He grabbed the tool and vanished back into the console.

'Watch it, we've got a pumper.' Conaway dropped the needle and stuck out her hand peremptorily. 'Cauteriser.' She grabbed the instrument and began to work on the artery. 'Anyone know the Kyrie from Fauré's *Requiem*?' She sang as she worked and smiled as she sang.

The Doctor's hand emerged from the console again. 'Tyre lever.' His head emerged briefly, just long enough to glance at the approaching rock and grin reassuringly at his startled audience. 'Anyone know the Kyrie from Fauré's *Requiem*?' He sang as he worked, his voice emerging with a nasal timbre, and flat, from the innards of the console.

The clatter of debris against the ship's hull beat an unusual but not inappropriate accompaniment.

To this somewhat less than sacred rendition of the Doctor's favourite piece of sacred music, the asteroid defence systems sprang eagerly to life and, to the sound of spontaneous applause from the bridge officers, blew the approaching rock into an countless number of mostly harmless pieces.

The Doctor extracted himself from the console, closed the hatch, glanced in minor puzzlement at the double handful of circuit boards he was still holding, shrugged, stuffed them in his pockets and beamed at the console operator beside him. 'Soft centre,' he snapped, holding out his hand and waggling the fingers impatiently. 'A congratulatory coffee cream I think. Have one yourself.' Munching happily, he retrieved his tools from the console operator and stuffed them back into his pocket with the already forgotten circuit boards.

He looked at Captain Bellis and grinned with immense satisfaction, much as she imagined a small boy would grin after finding something utterly unsavoury in the local tip, while showing off afterwards to his mates about how tasty it was.

'How did you do that?' Bellis couldn't stop the question coming out in a rather high-pitched voice.

'Oh… you know.' The Doctor shrugged modestly. 'Centuries of life experience, a degree in the psychology and social dynamics of machine intelligence, a two-week apprenticeship at Kwik-Fit…'

Bellis stared. 'And what about the engines?'

'Engines?' The Doctor stopped in mid-chew with a second coffee cream halfway to his mouth. 'Nobody mentioned anything was wrong with the *engines*.'

On any normal day the surface of the southern hemisphere of Belannia VI was generally considered even more attractive up close than it was from orbit. The ocean was a deep tropical blue and sprinkled with a fine dusting of gorgeous atolls. The fish went quietly about their business and the sea-birds were busy poking their noses – and beaks – into it.

A normal day.

Today, however, was, most assuredly, anything but a normal day.

Five hundred kilometres closer to the equator than the capital city was a chain of mildly active but nonetheless beautiful volcanic islands, scallop-shaped cones of volcanic pumice with hot sandy beaches and abundant wildlife produced regularly whenever the local tectonic plates could not decide which had the more legitimate claim on the surrounding geological area. Local conditions, therefore, were seldom what might be considered temperate. Today, however, was a day that would put even the most violently active of geological events into the shade.

There had been indications of the approaching planetary disaster for some time but these had gone largely unnoticed by the local population of holidaying Belannian politicians and statesmen who were, in the main, here to get away from the stress and bustle of their everyday lives.

The first *major* indication that there was trouble afoot – on a scale that would make the problems of Noah seem like so many bathtime fairy tales – was when a large spacecraft carrying several thousand refugees fell crazily out of orbit and smashed into the ocean, producing a shockwave that killed ocean and sky dwellers alike for some very considerable distance from the site of impact.

The second major indication was when several large chunks of Belannia VI's moon began rapidly to follow suit.

His name was Father Alexis Denadi, and he was a priest. It had taken Sam a while to figure this out. What she thought were a cowl and habit had in fact been the loose plastic folds of an emergency environment suit. As the air pressure reached dangerously low levels he had taken another suit and bundled her into it. The suits were very little more than basic life-support mechanisms – they had small emergency beacons but no radios.

With the air gone Sam had no choice but to follow the priest through the still-shaking outer suburbs of the city in the hope of finding an area that still held pressure.

For Sam, the journey had been a shocking experience. As if the shaking of the ground and the almost continuous collapse of the buildings between which they moved wasn't enough, she also had to contend with the bodies. There were so many, those who had not made it clear of the depressurising section of the city. They were mostly adults, but some children lay scattered across her path, bodies bloated and bruised from internal haemorrhaging, limbs outstretched as if grasping for life, or curled around themselves as if attempting desperately to prevent its escape.

Sam had no clear idea how long the journey had taken. She didn't become aware that the air in her emergency suit was becoming stale and hot until Father Denadi took her by the shoulders and unzipped the helmet. Only as she breathed in fresh air laced with the scent of damp grass and pond flowers did she realise that the tiredness and blurred vision that she had been experiencing were due not to exhaustion but to oxygen deprivation.

She began to take off the suit. Father Denadi placed a hand on her arm, stopping the movement. He unzipped his own helmet, and his expression told Sam that they weren't out of the woods yet. This much was true, Sam realised. The ground underneath her feet was still shaking. All right, the movement wasn't as strong as before but it was definitely there, and showed no signs of going away.

Sam's eyes remained fixed on Father Denadi's craggy face as she became aware of voices surrounding her. She caught her breath and looked around. She was in another park. This one was much smaller than the one in which she had nearly been killed, more a kind of ornamental garden really. Small trees that looked a bit like weeping willows formed arches of rustling green across a transparent roof through which the stars shone unchangingly. Ornamental bushes wound between the willows in a leafy maze. A pond bordered with cracked stone flagging snaked between the bushes. As the ground shook, water slopped over the stone and soaked into the grass, carrying with it a bedraggled tide of lily pads. Between the trees, Sam could see the shattered remains of a number of buildings, their jagged stumps lit by fitfully flickering windows, their upper ramparts silhouetted against the bulk of the grey-green planet she had seen earlier, itself now shrouded in darkness and reduced to a thick crescent by its own advancing terminator.

Sitting or standing nearby were a group of perhaps twenty or thirty people. They were huddled together beneath the largest of the willows, whose branches scraped and swayed above them. The sound she had heard was that of their devotions. Their voices were low, continuous, a fog bank of prayer drifting through trees and across the damp grass.

Sam felt something scuttle across her foot and jumped. She looked down. A frog. She sat down suddenly on the grass, put her head in her hands and began to giggle. The giggles quickly turned into laughter, the laughter to tears. She screwed her eyes tightly shut and knuckled her fists against her eyelids, trying to shut out the memory of the faces of the people she had passed, the people who had not made it to the garden, and life. She wondered briefly how many other pockets of people there were in the city, trapped in areas of pressure, isolated from death by the thickness of a wall or window, waiting in fear for the trembling of the ground to increase again to killing strength.

Sam did not know how long she cried, only that she felt better when she stopped. Which was stupid when you thought about it – the ground was still shaking, the people were still praying. Only the frogs had gone.

She looked up. Father Denadi had joined the group of people and was moving among them, smiling, his presence clearly reassuring them. He touched the face of a young child and the child stopped crying. In fact, now that she noticed it, Sam was surprised to see that the people were in the main calm, almost tranquil. She saw none of the panic or fear she had witnessed in the last hours with those who had died. She got stiffly up from the damp grass and walked curiously towards the group. As she moved closer she realised that their numbers had increased. She saw other people emerging from between the trees and ornamental bushes: single adults, others with children, occasionally a lone, puzzled child; clumps of people who had clearly come into the garden from different entrances from the one she had used, and who were now moving to join the throng, drawn by the sound of prayer, the sound of peace among all the violence.

As Sam moved closer, she began to hear the words spoken by Father Denadi to the congregation – she found herself thinking of the group in that way – and she frowned.

'… death is among us… but do not fear… death is our friend… death frees us from the prison of our lives… death is the doorway to our Endless State…'

A large man dressed in a neat suit with a neatly trimmed beard said in a small voice, 'How do we know that we won't be left behind?'

Father Denadi smiled. 'For those with faith the doorway stands ever open. You may walk through it at any time.'

The man sighed with relief and began again to pray.

Father Denadi offered something to the large man. A votive wafer. Sam realised that a number of the group had similar wafers. The large man took the wafer from the priest. Sam thought she saw tears on the large man's cheeks as he placed it into his mouth and swallowed.

She moved closer. Father Denadi turned, saw her, waved her nearer still. 'Come,' he said. 'Join us.'

Sam hesitated.

Father Denadi took a step closer. His smile was tranquil yet something of the tranquillity struck Sam as infinitely threatening. She took a step back.

'You are scared.'

'You're right there! We're in the middle of an earthquake, the city's falling down and God knows how many people have died already…'

Sam became aware that the people had fallen silent around her, their prayers dissolving into startled muttering. A child pointed at her. 'She used the G-word!'

Sam glanced around. Suddenly the group of people seemed more like a crowd. A crowd whose attention had been directed at her.

A woman said, quietly, 'You sound as if you doubt your Endless State.'

Another said, 'Why are you here if you're not a believer?'

The large man who had eaten the wafer gazed at her with limpid eyes. The eyes were half closed. There was no pain on his face as he sank to his knees and curled up on the wet grass, as if to sleep.

Sam began to shake.

The people moved closer, slowly, almost unobtrusively, drifting as their prayers had drifted across the wet grass. All except the very large man and a few others she now realised also remained motionless on the grass.

Sam blinked. She was surrounded. There was nowhere to run. The air in her suit was gone. These people… what did they want with her?

'We can help you,' said the woman.

'If you'll let us,' said a teenage boy.

'All you have to do is believe.'

'Believe in what?' Sam pointed at the motionless form of the large man. 'Having a snooze while your city falls down around your ears?'

The woman bestowed upon Sam an utterly beautiful smile. 'Oh my poor child. He's not asleep. He's Endless.' The word was said with a reverence that made Sam think it could not possibly be uttered with a small 'e'.

A man said loudly, 'If you do not want to be Endless you should not be here. Our State is our choice. You choose to live in a prison. We choose to free ourselves from that prison. Now the time is right to attain our Endless State.'

The capital letters again. Sam felt herself shaking. Her foot slipped on the grass. She turned, half fell, found herself on her knees as the crowd finally reached her, hands reaching out to touch her, but gently, caressingly, the voices a gestalt sigh.

'– help you, we can –'

'– must have come here for a reason, why else –'

'– attain your Endless State if you only –'

'– just don't know it yet –'

'– let us help you –'

'– trust us –'

'– let us –'

'*No!*' Father Denadi's voice was a quiet thunder in the garden. He stepped between Sam and the crowd. 'I did not bring her here to force her but to educate her.' He looked at Sam. 'To save her.'

Sam glanced at the figure of the large man curled up asleep on the grass. No, she finally realised, not asleep. Something far worse. Far, far worse. 'You're mad. You killed that man. You gave him something to eat and now look at him, *just look at him*! He's just… lying there… in the wet… he doesn't… he's not… not even…'

breathing he's not

'… going to move if… when the rescue ships come.'

Father Denadi held out his hands comfortingly. Sam shied away from them. 'The rescue ships have already gone.' Sam gaped. 'There were twenty-five million people on this moon. How many ships do you suppose they would need to move us all?'

'Surely there must be…' Sam tailed off helplessly. 'I mean, they wouldn't just abandon you… I mean, they wouldn't, would they? People just don't do that…' She looked around uncertainly as her words trailed away. 'Do they?'

'The disasters continue on other worlds in our system. Belannia VI and Belannia VIII. Our resources are limited. The Hanakoi will not help. The Hoth are meditating. Meanwhile our Sign has come. The Message.' Father Denadi pointed up out of the transparent roof of the garden. Sam followed his pointing finger. She looked past the swaying branches of the willows. He seemed to be pointing at the Belannian sun, which was flickering as it edged around the disc of Belannia VI. No, not flickering, she realised suddenly. Stars don't *flicker*. Not unless they're quasars or binaries or –

– *unless they were unstable in some way.*

Some way that was causing the destruction she had seen.

What was it with suns these days? She thought of the near-disasters Janus had brought about, and wondered if the Belannian sun was being manipulated in the same way.

And what the hell can I do about it even if it is? she thought.

Father Denadi said quietly, 'Behold the sun, Bel, is our Sign. Our inescapable Message. It is our time now. And yours. Join with us. Embrace your Endless State.'

'No! You are wrong!'

The voice was deep, the effect on the congregation that of nails scraped across a board. The man who stepped from the crowd must once have been horribly burnt. His skin held the faint sheen of scar tissue, his eyes the terrible brightness of obsession. 'You do not understand. You are misguided. The girl is right. Nobody has to die. I, Saketh, was once a believer. I listened to the teachings, and the words were more than comfort to me. But that was before I found the Truth. The Truth is not Endless in the way you think. I know. For...' He hesitated, his eyes lost in distant memories of pain and revelation. When he continued his voice was dusted with ecstasy. 'I have attained my Endless State. I have attained it here, in *Life*.'

The crowd murmured angrily at his words.

'He mocks us!'

'Blasphemer!'

'Attain the Endless State? In Life? Impossible!'

'Mummy, he used the D-word!'

Sam stared around her wildly. 'You're *all* mad!' she cried. 'There are ships at the spaceport. In a city this size there must be!'

Father Denadi said brusquely, 'The spaceport is unreachable without spacesuits. Most here do not have them. Those that do do not have enough air.' Turning his attention to the newcomer, he added, 'Brother Saketh, you came to me not two months ago and swore that your time had come and you would attain your Endless State.'

'And I have!'

'*Do not lie to me brother!*' Denadi's voice was a roar. 'The Endless State is unattainable in Life. The Scriptures tell us it is so. "First shall there be freedom from the prison of life, then shall come the attainment of Endlessness." '

'And so it is.' Saketh's eyes shone with religious fervour. 'The difference is only in emphasis. I have died, and returned. Now I am Endless!' He looked wildly from person to person, marched right up to Father Denadi and thrust his scarred face into that of the priest. 'I shall prove it to you!'

And he turned, thrusting his way through the crowd, elbowing people aside as he walked through the trees towards the nearest wall. The wall was transparent – Sam could see the archway of an emergency airlock set into it. Saketh opened the inner door and stepped in. The crowd had fallen silent, waiting.

A child said, 'Daddy, what –' and was impatiently shushed.

Father Denadi made the Sign of the Ankh and sighed. 'Saketh will attain his Endless State.'

Sam gazed at the priest in horror. 'He's not wearing a spacesuit! You saw those people we passed! He'll die!'

Father Denadi gazed levelly at her. 'He will become Endless.'

Sam felt something snap in her head. 'That's a load of crap!' She ran clumsily in her spacesuit towards the airlock. She banged on the wall. Saketh turned to her and smiled. His face was torn and ugly, yet somehow peaceful, even... *beautiful*? The shock of the expression drove Sam back from the wall.

And then Saketh opened the outer airlock door and stepped out on to the airless surface.

He fell.

46

Sam covered her eyes. Tried not to imagine what was happening to his eyes and lungs and blood vessels, his skin, his ears, his *mind*.

There was a moment of silence and then she heard a loud gasp from the congregation behind her. She turned, opened her eyes. As one, they were staring past her, out of the garden. Some of the children were pointing. She turned back to the wall.

On the surface – the *airless surface* – of Belannia VI's moon, Saketh was *standing up*.

He turned, his face creased with pain. She could see bruises erupting through the newly healed skin of his face and hands. He lifted the hands, turned them, examined them, found them good. He held them out to her, to all of them, a silent messiah, inexplicably, impossibly alive in a landscape that clearly held only death for anyone else.

Saketh opened the airlock and came back in. He was shaking, clearly racked with pain. The bruising alone, indication of internal injuries, must have been excruciating. But why wasn't he dead?

Sam got no answer to this question, though she could see his bruises shifting and fading, inexplicably quickly.

The people were looking at Saketh with silent, stunned awe. Father Denadi was all but forgotten. 'I offer you myself. I offer you life,' he was saying.

When Saketh spoke, his voice was the grinding rattle of broken machinery. He turned to Denadi and took the wafers he had been handing out to the crowd. 'We all know what these wafers contain.'

The listeners sighed. Sam looked at the very large man still lying on the ground. Someone said, 'They contain our Choice. The attainment of our Eternal State.'

Saketh hissed, 'No! They contain poison. Those that eat of this bread will attain nothing but death.'

If anyone else had been speaking this would have been too much for the crowd. Saketh held them, however, with his bruised face and bloodshot eyes.

And then he ate a wafer.

They waited.

His face twisted slightly, then returned to its bruised placidity. He did not fall.

The crowd sighed.

He took a number of the wafers, placed them briefly into his mouth and then restacked them in his palm. 'I have eaten the bread and still I live!' He licked cracked lips, continued in a hushed voice, 'I have transmuted death to life.' His voice rose to a crescendo as he added, 'Whomsoever follows me and eats of my flesh will live for ever. They will have their Eternal State while in this life – *and life itself will no longer be a prison!*' He glanced at Father Denadi, who was on his knees, eyes jammed shut, praying devoutly. 'I shall not lie to you. It will hurt.' His eyes closed momentarily, lost in memories, 'Oh yes, more than you can imagine... but... follow me and I will save you all.'

He fell silent and waited. Then a child stepped forward, wrenching itself free of its parent to run to Saketh. 'Want to live!' said the child. 'Scared. Want to go home now!' Hesitantly the parents followed. Saketh offered them the wafers and they took them.

'No!' Father Denadi was on his feet, moving, swiping the wafers from their hands and crushing them in a fist, his voice loud and righteous in the shocked stillness. 'He has corrupted the attainment of your Endless State. If you eat of his bread you will be damned to hell!'

The parents looked at Father Denadi as the child stumbled back, clutching at its mother in fear.

'You see what you do to them? How you frighten them?' Saketh's voice was calm, the previous raspiness fading even as Sam thought to listen for it. Father Denadi stopped. He looked at the people. They were scared. Of him. He turned, his face flushed with shame. He looked around slowly. No one would meet his gaze. He knew what they wanted and he could not give it to them. Shoulders slumped, he moved slowly off into the trees. Sam heard him praying there like a big old bear grumbling tiredly to itself.

The parents returned their attention to Saketh. He offered them more wafers. They took one each, gave one to their child. They put them into their mouths and swallowed.

Saketh's voice rose in exultation. 'From this moment on, cities, moons, planets are as nothing. You cannot die. Vacuum, radiation, poison – none of these can affect your Endless State. You will live for ever. *The universe is your home!'*

The crowd surged toward Saketh, who raised his bruised arms to bestow a benediction upon them. Sam shuddered. No matter how hard she tried to convince herself it had all been a trick, an elaborate hoax, she could not escape the feeling she had just seen something being born, something that would change everything. She was terrified, sweating, sick to her stomach with the sudden emotion churning in the garden. She backed slowly away as the crowd swelled around Saketh. She turned, rubbing her eyes as if to keep tears from her face.

A few moments later the airlock cycled several times. Sam was alone in the garden.

No, she suddenly remembered – not alone after all.

She began to follow the sound of Father Denadi's prayers into the rustling depths of the trees, her feet moving uncertainly upon the still-shaking, increasingly unstable ground.

* * *

49

The Doctor stood upon the lava shield of the young volcano watching people chopping trees with desperate abandon. He studied the beach, which lay perhaps a quarter of a mile away, and reformulated his previous definition of the area – as a collection of various geological formations concealing numerous species of biological life assaulted continuously by liquid in a high-energy state – to include the additional but highly important phrase: assaulted by fragments of lunar debris in a high-energy state.

He wondered if Sam would be pleased by the more precise definition.

He thought possibly not. Especially since she had been on the moon in question. He thought about this for another few moments, wondering eventually why he was not more upset. Sentimentality. He'd always subscribed to it in the past. He cared about his compan– his friends, didn't he? Why did it seem so easy, then, sometimes, to put the emotion aside? To put *her* aside? He shook his head. Humans could do it. He noticed that they seemed to do it more often the older they got. Was he getting old? Was he becoming more human? Absorbing their mores and morals by some kind of osmosis?

There was no answer of course. At least none of either a definite or comforting nature. If Sam was dead… at least it had probably been quick. At least, he *hoped* it had been quick… The thought of her suffering…

He shook his head again, this time to dislodge some fairly unpleasant images.

He looked more closely at the beach. The three sections of the medical frigate lay like beached whales upon the shore. A hundred or so people were siting or standing nearby. Behind them the ocean rolled away to a grey and listless horizon. Clouds were gathering there in a rolling front, obscuring the sun – which,

50

he had been aware for some time, was fluctuating in brightness in the slightly disconcerting way in which normal main-sequence stars generally don't.

He wondered vaguely if the TARDIS had got a bee in her bonnet about wayward suns at the moment. As she got older, she seemed to be getting more eccentric. Or perhaps it was deliberate. Perhaps the more he tried to be the aimless wanderer, the more she was gently asserting herself, working to her own agenda.

He frowned. That bothered him a little.

The rest of the refugees were working in the forests covering the lower slopes of the volcano. They were chopping trees and they were doing it at his suggestion. Trees made good rafts. Rafts might save them all from the tsunami he knew was coming.

He shielded his eyes as more burning debris dropped through the roiling cloud layer and smashed into the ocean. Belannia VI was a large world, twice as big as Sam's Earth, but it was considerably less dense, and with lower gravity. The movement of the ocean was slower, dreamier, but nonetheless just as deadly. The Doctor had been watching rock fall out of the sky for several hours. The last piece to survive re-entry had been large – dangerously large. He'd made what he thought was a fairly accurate guess of its trajectory and mass and then, with a charming smile to allay the fears of the refugees, suggested that they might like to begin chopping down the trees.

That had been an hour ago. Then the sky had been brilliant with sun, filled with little fluffy clouds, swimmingly hazy mirages of other nearby atolls and the blankly incurious cries of sea birds who by then were beginning to get used to the idea of a spaceship lying wrecked on their island. Now the birds had prudently flown away while the sun glimmered only fitfully through a sky the colour of welded metal, hard and grey with little coloured bits dancing around on the edges of his vision. The little coloured bits were the most worrying. They gave a very firm indication of the water content in the sky, the water content being indicative of light refraction. And there were rather a lot of little coloured bits. And they were getting closer.

There was a lot of water heading towards the island. Several million tons. A tsunami.

You can't throw chunks of moon at a planet, no matter the size, without its having some effect on the local geography.

The Doctor checked his pocket watch. He flipped open the lid, smiled dreamily at the bright musical chime from within, then snapped it shut. He hopped from rock to rock, bouncing around the lava shield, encouraging the cutters to work harder and helping those moving the logs to drag them with even greater speed down to the beach.

At the beach Captain Bellis was supervising the unsnapping of the medical frigate's three remaining lifeboats. One was already on the shore, one was being hoisted clear of the wreckage and a third was still jammed inside a buckled section of hull. Moving straight to the beached lifeboat, the Doctor rubbed his hands together with glee.

Surgeon Major Conaway stopped him a few yards from the hull. 'Thinking of leaving us? I wouldn't blame you. But the lifeboat will only take fifty or so people. How do you choose who will stay and who will go?'

The Doctor cracked his knuckles like a concert pianist about to perform a particularly tricky recital. 'Hm. Logical assumption under the circumstances, if a bit cynical. But, all things being equal, we're not going to leave anyone behind.'

'How are you going to get lifeboats with space for a hundred and fifty people to hold ten times that number?'

The Doctor examined the engine cowling of the lifeboat, cocked his head, considered, thumped the release and then stood clear as the hatch cover opened. 'Have you ever heard the phrase, "If the mountain won't come to Mahomet"?'

'So?'

The Doctor ducked into the engine compartment. 'Well, that was a saying coined by a man who clearly had no understanding of gravitational-transference engineering.' Conaway blinked. The Doctor popped his head out again and grinned at her. 'How would you like to assist me in a different kind of operation?' The childlike excitement in his voice suggested to the surgeon major that it wasn't a question of life and death, more a kind of invitation to dance.

Conaway found herself smiling. Which was utterly insane considering their predicament, and what she thought of this amazingly bizarre man and the incredibly irresponsible thing she was about to do. 'All right,' she said with a mystifying lack of hesitation.

'Wonderful, wonderful. Now I don't know about you but I like a little music while I work. Do you know the Kyrie from Fauré's *Requiem*?' He rummaged in his pocket, pulled out a battered old harmonica and, pausing only to grab the lifeboat toolkit, dived head first back into the engine compartment.

The Doctor's plan was interrupted first when the third lifeboat fell on Captain Bellis while it was being hoisted free of the wrecked ship.

The Doctor had got as far as disassembling the engine mounting and ordering the laying out in rows of the hundred or so tree trunks which were the first to arrive on the beach. When the winch arm broke the Doctor did not wait for the scream before patting Conaway on the shoulder and taking the toolkit from her. 'They're going to need you,' he said sombrely.

Conaway sent a nurse back within moments. 'It's Captain Bellis. She's trapped under the winch arm and some broken hull plates. We can't get her out because the plates are too heavy to move and the winch is broken. The surgeon major said to tell you she "wants the bloody mountain and wants it bloody now". Her exact words.' The nurse's quiet look suggested she did not hold out much hope for Captain Bellis – or Surgeon Major Conaway – if she persisted in using highly qualified personnel as message-carriers for this strange man with his head buried in the lifeboat engine compartment.

For his part the Doctor merely smiled a terse smile. 'Do we have five minutes?'

'We have as many as you want,' said the nurse. 'Captain Bellis doesn't.'

The Doctor nodded, sucked on the end of a screwdriver and dived back into the engine compartment. 'I'll be there in three,' he said.

And so he was – nursemaiding a strange metallic shape which hovered in the air beside him. He guided the mass of equipment through the crowd of people, along the beach to where a number of medics clustered beside the largest of the wrecked sections of spacecraft, and called out for Conaway.

'In here.' The surgeon major's voice rumbled out of the depths with a peculiar metallic echo. 'And be careful. This whole lot is balanced so finely one good sneeze could bring it down.'

The Doctor wriggled into the gap between two fractured metal hull plates, slipped sideways and continued his journey down. 'Ah,' he said when he reached the end of the channel. Conaway and two nurses were busy hunched over the crumpled form of

Captain Bellis, who was trapped within the winch cabin, which was pinned beneath a section of hull. More bent sections fenced off the winch and sealed the cabin door shut. They could reach her by wriggling through the wreckage, but they couldn't get her out. Conaway fastened a drip into one arm and managed to turn to face the Doctor. 'She was using the winch. The section of hull it was fastened to collapsed. The whole lot caved in with her inside. We've got a drip into her but she's bleeding. I can't reach the site of the injury. We need to get her out.'

The Doctor was nodding. 'Yes, yes, I see... uh huh... yes...' He began to wriggle backwards.

Conaway said, 'Got any bright ideas?'

'Oh... one or two, one or two.' The Doctor continued to wriggle. A few moments later he was standing back outside the ship. He ran to the still-hovering mass of equipment. 'Now then... calculating the tonnage... moment of inertia... coefficient of friction... I would imagine it would be the... *yellow* button.'

He pushed a button then jumped as the sudden crack of tearing metal came from within the wreck.

The medics and refugees standing nearby looked at him sharply, backing away from the wreck. He offered them a brightly reassuring grin, which completely failed to reassure them.

The hovering equipment began to emit a high-pitched whine. Smoke wafted gently from its interior. It grew hot. The air crackled with ionisation. A tiny rainbow formed above the machine and drops of rain fell upon it, hissing – or rather they did not fall upon it. The Doctor was delighted to see that the drops did not actually touch the casing of the equipment. Instead they stopped, hovered impossibly a centimetre or two above the metal, spun in dizzying circles, and then flung themselves back skywards again at great speed, as if terribly embarrassed to be caught doing something that no self-respecting matter, even matter such as that which composed rain, had any right to do.

And then with less fuss than a seagull taking advantage of a local updraft, the upper half of the medical frigate, a weight of approximately twenty-five thousand tons of metal, rose smoothly, silently and effortlessly, three metres into the air.

The medics ran forward into the now accessible hulk, rushing to help Conaway and her team start to free Captain Bellis from the wreckage.

It was while the medics were doing this that some refugees noticed what was to be the second interruption in the Doctor's plan – darkening the horizon in a line of charcoal grey against the lighter grey sky was the first of the gigantic waves that the Doctor had been expecting.

He watched the wave approach as he waited for the medics to bring Captain Bellis from the wreck. A moment passed. Another. Neither medics nor patient appeared. Beside the Doctor the makeshift lash-up of equipment he had constructed from the lifeboat's engine began to shake. It grew hotter, and even more smoke issued from it. Three metres above the space where the medics were working a mass of metal weighing twenty-five thousand tons began to hover as if considering seriously what it was doing there and why, and how, and, more importantly, why it should not actually assume its previous position much closer to the ground.

Between the two jagged masses of metal the tidal wave moved swiftly towards the beach. Already the Doctor could see it was several kilometres closer than when he had last looked. The hundred or so refugees ranged along the beach began to run towards the tree line grabbing possessions or children, whichever happened to be closer, as they did so.

The Doctor glanced from the hovering contraption beside him back into the wreck of the medical frigate. Where were the medics? Where was Conaway? Where was Captain Bellis? With a reassuring pat which resulted in a painful yelp and the sucking of burnt fingers the Doctor left his machine, ran across the beach and into the wreck.

A moment later he was standing beside a group of medics crouched over Captain Bellis. Her clothes were soaked with blood. She was moaning, her body struggling against the pain of her injuries.

'Shears! Get her uniform off. We have to find out where the blood's coming from.'

A moment later one of the nurses had broken out the field steriliser and was handing instruments to Conaway.

'Excuse me', said the Doctor. 'I don't know if now's quite the right time –'

'Clean! I need her clean. I can't see what the hell I'm doing.' Conaway looked up in considerable irritation. 'Water. Where the hell's the water?'

The Doctor pointed towards the tidal wave which, although it was yet only cresting the horizon, must already have been looming several hundred metres above them. 'I rather think there's more water there than you're quite capable of dealing with.'

Conaway did not look up. 'She's bleeding internally. If we move her, she's dead.'

The Doctor nodded. 'If we don't move her, she'll drown. And so will we.' He glanced back over his shoulder at the machine, which was now shaking dramatically and emitting colourful showers of sparks. 'It might on the other hand,' said the Doctor with a glance up towards the huge tonnage of metal hanging a metre or so above his head, which was also shaking, 'be a dilemma that could well be redundant in another minute or two anyway.' And he swept aside the nurses, picked up Captain Bellis as if she were a rag doll and began to run back through the wreck.

Conaway swore. The rest of the medics glanced at the looming tidal wave, then turned to run after the Doctor. Gathering what equipment she could, Conaway followed.

The Doctor ran through the jagged maze of the wreck, leaping from hull plate to buckled hull plate, feet booming on the wreckage. Above his head the hovering mass of additional wreckage began to squeal. Bits of it suddenly began to fall, jagged slivers and chunks of metal lancing down to form a shifting maze through which the Doctor ran. He was aware of the medics moving less quickly behind him. He called instructions to them above the screech, directing them through the shifting maze of metal he himself was still navigating. 'Conaway, go left. No, right now, straight on, jump, right, left, jump, jump, now *run*!'

They ran.

The wave grew higher, closer. The jagged ceiling dropped until the Doctor was forced to run almost doubled over, making the task of carrying Bellis even more arduous. He was still calling instructions to the medics. All around him metal was slamming against metal; his ears rang with the sound so he damped their input. He pitched his voice above the concussion of debris and kept yelling instructions.

A moment later he burst from the wreckage on to the beach. He gently laid Captain Bellis on the shore and ran to the machine. It was throbbing, shaking, screeching with a demented electronic hum. Bits of equipment were shaking loose. One or two had already fallen off. 'Oh,' the Doctor said quickly, considering the detached items while working to hold the rest together. 'Well, maybe I didn't need those after all.' He glanced over the machine and then back at the trembling mass of hovering wreckage.

Then, making what might have seemed like the most insane decision in his life, the Doctor bolted back into the mass of wreckage.

The medics crawled and fell clear of the wreckage as the machine began to sputter. They stared back at the Doctor as he vanished into the wreckage. More metal fell as the Doctor's machine began to screech even more loudly. The Doctor reappeared, leapt clear of the battered hulk, and ran to his machine, stuffing something into his pocket as he did so.

He reached the machine. A batch of wires had pulled loose and was flapping around wildly, like a horse lashing its tail at flies. The Doctor spared the wave a glance and thought the analogy particularly apt. The wave had sucked away the ocean, revealing a coral shoreline which extended perhaps half a kilometre from the beach. The wave was already peeling across this newly exposed stretch of beach, curling and still rising. The Doctor's hands were a blur as he grasped the shaking machine and tried to reprogram it. He could not operate the controls because they were shaking so violently. Impatiently he slapped at a large red palm-sized button and, after three attempts, managed to hit it. The machine shut down and fell on to the beach with a jarring thud. A split second later twenty-five thousand tons of metal smashed together with an awesome impact behind him.

Debris flew everywhere. The air crackled with the pressure of the approaching wave. The medics clustered around the machine, hushed and terrified. Only Conaway thought to attempt to stop Bellis bleeding. The Doctor began to reprogram the machine, his hands a blur across the controls, jamming leads back in here, tucking small items of equipment back into the chassis there. At various times he seemed to be holding pliers, spanner, screwdriver, spot welder, circuit tester, eyeglass, tweezers, Johnson's cotton buds, various electronic probes and at least once his formidable-looking set of tyre levers. Nobody was watching. Their total attention was fixed on the mountain of water roaring unstoppably towards the beach.

Then it hit, smashing against the shore, cresting across the mass of wreckage which had once been a spaceship and blasting it into deadly jagged missiles. It smashed against the beach, ripping up chunks of coral as big as houses and flinging them across the tree line. The sound was like a continuous blast of thunder. Beside the Doctor everyone was screaming or shouting – it made no difference: their voices were gone, whirled away in the maelstrom of sound in the split second before the wave smashed into the island.

The Doctor was punching controls on the device he had made when the wave hit.

Or rather *didn't* hit.

For, as the machine leapt back into protesting life, the wave – all several thousand tons of it – simply didn't get any lower than about thirty metres. It washed over them, hovering just above the tops of the palm trees edging the beach. The Doctor sighed. He looked up at the watery roof hanging over the island. The water itself was still moving at tremendous speed, smashing with all the force of enraged nature against the invisible barrier. The machine began to shake again. It was putting out an awful lot of energy. Far more than it had when supporting the wreckage of the ship. But fortunately it would have to last only a few minutes this time. The Doctor looked out across the beach. The sand, the trees, everything was coloured a muddy green-brown by sunlight filtering through the wave hurtling past overhead. Further inland the tops of trees were neatly sliced off at lower and lower heights as they climbed the volcano slopes. The volcano itself vanished into the water as a rippling cone of rock and trees. The wave spread itself thinly across the force field at this point, allowing more sunlight to fall through. The quality of the light was for a few moments some of the most glorious the Doctor had ever seen, as if the forest, even the island itself, were inside a giant cathedral whose walls were made of water instead of stone. A slow smile spread dreamily across his face. His eyes crinkled. Thoughts chased themselves through his head in disconnected streams.

Beside him the machine emitted a single embittered sigh and shut down. The Doctor glanced upward in alarm. Fortunately the wave had almost completely passed, but it rained pretty starfish and hideous smelling seaweed for almost five minutes.

Conaway had not stopped working on Captain Bellis. The Doctor would not have been surprised to learn she hadn't even noticed the wave as it passed overhead. Now she looked up. 'She'll live.'

The Doctor nodded, pleased. He looked around and found a number of medical staff staring at him. A nurse marched up to him, grabbed him by the collar and yanked him off his feet. 'We could have died! Your machine saved us! *Why did you go back into the wreckage?*'

The Doctor blinked, rummaged in his pocket, drew forth a battered piece of paper. 'Captain Bellis dropped this. A family snapshot, I presume. I thought she might like to see it when she recovered.'

The nurse gazed at the Doctor in astonishment bordering on insanity. 'You're mad,' he whispered, letting the Doctor regain his footing. The Doctor waited but there was no apology. The nurse simply turned and walked away.

The Doctor pursed his lips sadly. A moment passed. He became aware of a presence beside him. Conaway was looking out to sea, to a second huge wave gathering on the horizon. At a rough guess this wave was twice as large as the first. 'We need to get off this island. How the hell are we going to do that?'

The Doctor glanced from the dripping remains of the weed-covered machine to the second lifeboat salvaged from the medical frigate where it had come to rest with other wreckage high up in the tree line. His eyes alighted on the smashed tree trunks, which added their lengths to those already brought from inland, and a wild light shone behind his eyes as connections, formed some while before, began to solidify.

'Tell me, Surgeon Major,' he said with a grin, 'have you ever had occasion to "catch the perfect wave"?'

Sully s'Vufu ignored the demands of her staff to *get to the hoverlite, Madam President, we have to leave now!* She knew she had to get clear of the city. She owed it to her government and to the people who had elected her to office. But, staring out of the picture window of the Greyhouse's Octagon stateroom at the approaching mountain of water which towered over the city, she found she could not in all conscience abandon her people to their fate.

'I'm not coming,' she said simply.

Her aide all but wrenched at her arm. 'Are you mad?' His voice was a hysterical screech. 'We have to get to the ship.'

'I put my faith in God,' she said. 'The God who placed me here in this room, here in this office, this position of responsibility. I cannot abandon my people.'

The aide blinked, jumping from one foot to the other. 'Madam President, if there's one thing I can guarantee you it is that you will be *bugger all use to your people when you are dead!* So please will you just come with me now to the hoverlite and we can get to the ship before it's too late?'

A half-smile played about her lips as she turned from the window. 'Geoffran,' she said, and her voice melted him, as it always did, 'we've known each other a long time. And there's no time to discuss this, you know that. No more afternoon tea and theosophical chats over iced biscuits. I cannot go. You on the other hand can – and must.' She touched his cheek fondly. 'If you don't, who will look after my successor?'

He gulped.

'What do you want me to tell Catheline and Jonaghan?'

'Tell them I love them. Tell them I hope that one day they will understand what I did and the reasons I did it. And give them these, for me will you?' She opened a drawer and brought out two small gift-wrapped packages. 'A word of advice. Never forget your children's birthdays.'

Geoffran wiped a tear from his cheek, took the packages and ran from the room.

She turned to face the wave. It curled above the city and its noise drowned the screaming of the people, the crashing of vehicles, the roar of the hoverlite's engines as it took off from the Octagon roof. The building was shaking with the force of the water. Plaster cracked from the ornamental ceiling and smashed against her desk, the Belannian flag set into the marbled floor. Plaster dusted her hair and the Arnelli rugs.

The wave grew higher. She could see vague shapes moving within it, hills and valleys of water glowing green and grey and sparkling in the brilliant sunlight.

She wondered how long it would take to reach her.

She wondered what it would feel like to die.

In front of the window, she got down on to her knees and began to pray.

A moment passed.

Another.

Her prayer finished, her thoughts moved to her children. Jonaghan, freckled, fair-headed like his father, Catheline, a bundle of flame-coloured hair topping a tranquil personality. Her kids were the best. Her life was the best. Nothing to do. No regrets. A curious calm stole over her. Gallows-calm she had heard it called. The moment before death. She looked up.

The wave had not moved.

She frowned.

The shaking had stopped.

She narrowed her eyes.

There was no sound at all.

Just a sigh of wind.

And a chirpy voice. 'Hm. Well, I'm sure there are many who would find such behaviour flattering but, really, there's no need to kneel.'

She refocused on the immediate landscape of the room. Hovering outside the window was a man. He had long hair and a smile as big and bright as the sun. She rose, inadvertently fulfilling his request, and took a step closer to the window. Ranged behind him was the most incredible sight she had ever seen. Fifteen hundred soaking-wet people stood or sprawled on a platform which seemed to be made of bits of wrecked machinery and several hundred *trees*. The... thing and the people... were hanging unsupported above the ground just below the level of the window.

'Who...?' she gasped. 'Who are you? How did you get here?'

The man offered his hand. 'That's a bit of an existential question, isn't it? I'm the Doctor.' He glanced back at the still-motionless wave. 'And obviously I surfed.'

Behind him, below the platform, a triumphant cheer rose from the city.

'Now, pardon me for being presumptuous but there are two rather important things we need to discuss. First, can we please have permission to land?'

'Of course. And second?'

'Well, it's a wee bit embarrassing, actually. I hardly care to mention it, except… well… except that I seem to have accumulated somewhere in the region of five hundred and eighty-three quadrillion ergs of potential energy that used to belong to that… er… wave over there. Now… I don't suppose you have anywhere I could, well, *put it all*, do you?'

Chapter Three

The capital world of the Bel system was a planet of light.

The northern hemisphere of Belannia VIII was currently shrouded in night, but millions of lights blazed in the darkness, sketching the skeletal shapes of cities and skyways, shining through a scattering of dark cloud in threads of fire, the connections of life across the planet never more easily shown.

Night here was a thing of legend, banished generations before by the combined efforts of the Hanakoi, to whom the Belannian refugees were now turning for help.

Help.

Not a thing to be lightly sought, nor easily given.

Not from the Hanakoi.

Father Denadi stood alone in the observation lounge of the private yacht pressed into refugee service by the Belannia VI government and stared out at the glimmering bulk of the planet that hung above him. He leaned against the window, resting his face against the glassite and trying not to surrender to the confusion he felt in his mind.

Alive.

Eldred Saketh was *alive*.

Father Denadi watched the lights of Belannia VIII brighten as the yacht dropped down from orbit and thought back to his first meeting with the man who had come back from a molten world on which he should have died. Father Denadi made the sign of the Ankh to atone for his blasphemous thought. Saketh should have attained his Endless State. Instead he'd apparently brought a blasphemous new religion to the people of Bel. A new religion for them – and fear for Father Denadi.

Fear was not a stranger. He had been taught to embrace it. To love it, to cherish it. Fear was the motivation that drove all to their Endless State. It was fear of life that drove them. Fear of death was no fear at all.

Denadi could not resist peeping out from beneath his acolyte's robes. The church was silent. All prayer was done now. The only sound was the sputtering of candles among the cold stone arches and the distant drone of the police flyers surrounding the church.

Twenty-three people sat, heads bowed, on the stone floor. Not for these the comforts of modern churches. No pews offered relief for tired muscles. Tiredness was a product of toxins, the pain bringing the acolytes one step closer to their Endless State.

The acolytes were young adults ranging from sixteen to twenty-five. They were silent now – not even their breath disturbed the chill stone grotto.

Denadi watched them. As he watched the Priest administer the last rites.

Saketh was a tall man, with piercing eyes and a neat beard. His body was taut; even beneath the robes he wore it seemed fit, a body that could carry a soul far indeed. For ever, maybe. When he broke the silence in prayer his voice was the roll of timpani, sunrise across noble mountains. His words went almost unnoticed among the rich timbre of that voice – but then it was not the words that were important. The words were simply the messengers. The message was the soul, the desire to attain Endlessness.

Outside the drone of police flyers increased.

A voice smashed into the cathedral silence: 'This is the Police.

You are in violation of State Order 173-A. You will now surrender to our authority.'

The drone of the Priest's voice did not falter. The congregation did not move.

The distorted voice from outside said, 'I repeat: you are in violation of State Order 173-A. Surrender now. Don't make us come in and get you, boys.'

Nothing. No movement, no sound beyond Saketh's voice. Then even that was gone.

A moment passed in silence.

The moment became one, two, five, ten.

No one spoke, no one breathed.

The congregation did not move.

Silence.

The wall exploded.

Fragments of stone fell around the congregation with a pall of smoke. They did not move. When police dressed in riot gear clambered into the church there were only two people left alive. Both were arrested. Denadi was given two years' hard labour followed by psychological counselling.

Saketh was charged with incitement to commit suicide.

He was sentenced to life.

Father Denadi was disturbed by the sound of somebody entering the observation lounge. He recognised the uncertain footsteps without having to turn around to look.

Sam moved alongside the priest, her attention also captured by the brilliantly lit planet above. 'Join the Dots,' she said staring at the densely packed lights of the many cities glowing through the clouds and streaking them with fire.

Father Denadi gave her a sideways glance. Sam let her eyes

flicker sideways briefly to meet his gaze.

'Dots,' she said. 'Join the Dots. I used to play it when I was a kid.' She searched the older man's face for any glimmer of expression. 'You never heard of Join the Dots?'

'I've no idea what you're…' Father Denadi's voice tailed off. He looked back out of the window at the planet. Sam waited to see if he would finish his sentence. He did not speak. Belannia VIII grew bigger, its curved edge flattening into a recognisable horizon.

'I was a child like you once.' The words were hushed, so quiet she almost missed them. The upper layers of threadlike clouds drifting past the window might have had more impact. 'I didn't know what I wanted. I didn't know who I was. And you know, I didn't care. Then I realised there were questions to be asked, answers to be sought. For a long time I thought I knew the best questions to ask. I thought I had the only answer I would ever need.'

Sam said quietly, 'You've played Join the Dots. You just don't like the picture you've made any more.'

Father Denadi made a curious sound – not quite a laugh and not quite a sigh. He shrugged ever so slightly. 'Saketh thinks he has found a new picture. He wants to show it to me. He wants to let me see.'

'The thing is,' said Sam, lifting her finger to poke at the window over the places where the city lights were moving slowly past, 'you can make any picture you like just by joining different dots. But the dots themselves don't change, do they?'

Again she waited for an answer. Clouds billowed up past the window and light from the cities streaked up through the clouds. Sam studied the lines and sharp planes of her companion's face and wondered if she ought to push the point. Father Denadi seemed like a man still searching for answers. She knew what that was like. She'd done quite a bit of searching for answers herself over the last few years. Her time spent away from the Doctor had shown her a fairly obvious truth, which was that being able to ask the right questions was often far more important than finding answers you couldn't use.

Sam smiled faintly as she found herself wondering how many other people had figured that out before her. Then she remembered the faces of those she had seen die, and stopped smiling. There were some things that made both question and answer – any question and answer – irrelevant.

'This is planet number eight, right? Where I come from we've only got one planet we can live on. How many planets are there in your solar system, anyway?'

'Twenty-three.'

'How many of them inhabited?'

'All of them except one,' said Father Denadi. 'The one to which we go to die,' and he made the sign of the Ankh.

Sam said, 'Belannia II, that's where Saketh went, isn't it? Have you ever thought about going there yourself?'

'I am not yet worthy to attain my Endless State.'

'You mean you're crapping yourself. Well, I would be, if I thought I was going to a place like that to die.'

Father Denadi did not reply.

Sam said brightly, 'But we're not, so that's OK, isn't it?'

Father Denadi continued to say nothing.

They stepped from the yacht on to the blasted concrete apron to the spaceport and into a dangerously large crowd of refugees. The sound was deafening, an incessant, insistent clamour for attention. People were shouting, arguing: demands for food, demands for shelter, worried interrogatives from displaced family members, the tearful crying or awful silence of children. Fearful mutterings, agonised groans, the full spectrum of negative emotions.

Sam felt herself taken by the arm and pulled around. A wild face with tear-grimed cheeks thrust close as a woman asked, 'Have you got any food? You must have some food. You must have something. What about your ship? You must have something on your ship. I've got money...' Grimy hands thrust forward, crumpled notes and sweaty coins protruding through clenched fingers. At that moment someone else knocked into the woman, who stumbled. Sam tried to steady the woman and was showered with coins as the woman fell screeching away.

The hubbub around her grew suddenly louder as more people pressed close with their own demands. Sam turned wildly this way and that, trying to find a way out of the crowd. But the crowd stretched as far as she could see, a sprawling log jam of restlessly turning heads, staring eyes, screaming mouths, waving hands, through which projected the metallic upper surfaces of berthed spacecraft. Even as she tried to get away she knew the task was hopeless. There was nowhere to get away *to*. She found herself having to lash out around her just to maintain her own breathing space.

And then something else was pushing her, a force she could not resist. Impossibly, a gap was opening in the crowd, an invisible force pushing aside adults and children alike, expanding waves of angry people squashed aside as the grime-streaked hull of a garbage scow tucked itself neatly into the resulting space and, pressor fields still grumbling on low power to hold back the crowd, began to disgorge even more refugees from its filthy interior.

Sam looked wildly around for Father Denadi. She could not see him. She cried out but could not even hear her own voice above that of the crowd. How could he hear her if she couldn't even hear herself? The stink from the garbage scow, added to the stink of the crowd, made her want to be sick. She had never considered herself either a claustrophobe or an agoraphobe but, well, this was different. This was both fears together – the fear of wide-open spaces jammed shoulder to shoulder with angry people.

Sam felt her breath catch in her throat. What was happening here? Why was everyone penned up like this? Why in the spaceport? Wasn't it dangerous? Why wasn't someone doing something about it? They couldn't just expect everyone to *stay* here. Several hundred metres away the grumble of a pressor field sank into the subsonic range of frequencies. Sam groaned and pressed her hands to her ears in pain. A moment later the sensation was gone and a metallic bundle of modules was rising gracefully into the night sky. The crowd bulged, flowed. Sam found herself in a river of people streaming into the space left by the ship.

What about radiation?

What about the subsonics?

What about the pressor fields?

Weren't they dangerous?

Wasn't anybody *ever* going to do anything?

Sam couldn't even tell if she was yelling her thoughts aloud rather than merely thinking them, so dense was the crowd and so great the noise and the fear that it generated. Already she was tired and wanted to sit down, but she knew if she did that she would be swept away or trampled underfoot. The crowd was like a big, slow animal, screeching for attention while it bumbled around looking for food, never realising that is was crushing its salvation underfoot.

As Sam felt she was going to lose it completely, a voice came to her above the sound of the crowd. '*Please remain calm.*' The voice was a magnified shriek, blasting down out of the sky. She looked up. A small blue and yellow vehicle hovered twenty or so metres above her head. '*This is a special message from the government of Belannia VIII. Due to the recent influx of refugees your ships have been rerouted to this holding area and you are to be billeted here for the duration of the emergency. Food and shelter will be provided shortly. Anyone with relatives on Belannia VIII or with recognised dual nationality or medical conditions requiring special treatment should make their way to the administration building in Sector 3-South-West-17.*'

'What about my children?' A voice yelled from some distance away. 'You can't expect children to stay in conditions like this!'

The voice, which Sam realised now must be a recorded message, continued without break: '*We apologise for the inconvenience. Please remain calm. This is a special message...*' The vehicle drifted on, the message repeating without variation as it passed slowly over the crowd.

Sam looked around. Where was Sector 3-South-West-17? And how could she reach it? And wouldn't it be full of people claiming sanctuary, seeking asylum or claiming medical conditions – anything to get out of the holding area?

She had to try. This was just like Ha'olam again. Wasn't she a refugee along with all the rest? Homeless? Alone?

Once again, she'd lost the Doctor, lost the sanctuary of the TARDIS. She cursed loudly.

And so she was back to square one: what should she do now she was here? Behave like a refugee or try to help? Wait patiently for someone else to solve the crisis so they could all go home? Subscribe to the anger and fear running riot here? Or try to sort things out? Improve the conditions here while she worked out a way of addressing the bigger picture?

It was no question when she got right down to it. Make a difference, Sam Jones.

To do that she had to get out of the system.

Out of the holding area.

She had to find Sector 3-South-West-17.

There were no signs in a spaceport, especially not on the landing apron. And even if there were she wouldn't be able to see them through all these people. Sam lowered her eyes to the ground. It was the one thing no one else was doing. They were all looking angrily at the sky, waving or shouting, trying to get the attention of the hovering vehicle. And so it was that Sam found herself looking at the very signpost for which she sought.

The ground was colour-coded. Arrows pointed to various sectors. Numbers delineated subsections within.

Sam grinned. She had a purpose now. She was beginning to feel better.

That was when she saw the blood.

She blinked. Spots of blood. Enough to frighten her again. Enough to make her realise how volatile the situation really was. Enough to make her realise how easy it was to fantasise, to carefully build a false view of things inside your own head until you couldn't tell which was real any more.

She cast around, following the blood, pushing back when she found herself in danger of being crushed or even attacked. Most people were just as frightened as she was. At the slightest sign of aggression they tended to back off. If they didn't, Sam just apologised, or turned and went another way. The psychos had enough people to pick a fight with. They could make do without her.

She found the source of the blood twenty minutes later. A boy, he must've been about eight. He was sitting on the ground near to a refuelling hatch which had been propped open by someone in the crowd. The hatch towered above the child, its greasy surface stinking of fuel. The little boy had been sick and was crying but was unable to leave the haven he had found himself in. He was sitting down on the refuelling nozzle's cap. His left leg was cut, quite deeply, the flesh bruised all around the knee. Sam wasn't sure the boy could walk. Blood caked his leg and hands, where he had rubbed the wound. Sam knelt quickly beside him, smiled a hello and examined the wound. 'Where's your mum?'

'Dunno.'

'What about your dad?'

'Dunno.'

'Do you have relatives here?'

'Dunno.'

'Is anyone looking after you?'

'Dunno.'

'What's your name?'

'Dunno.'

'I'm Sam.' She tried a smile. ' "Sam I am. Do you like green eggs and ham?" '

'Dunno.'

Sam sighed. She remembered Dan Engers, the boy she'd tried to look after on the *Cirrandaria*, and that in turn triggered another memory. 'When I was your age I used to read these books about a little boy like you. He was always getting into trouble and having adventures. His name was Danny. Danny Dunn. I'm going to call you Danny, OK?'

'OK.'

'So, Danny. Did you come in a spaceship?'

'S'pose so.'

'Where did you come from?'

'Dunno.' This time he grinned with her. 'My knee's killing me.'

Sam nodded thoughtfully. 'Can you walk?'

Danny shook his head. 'No way.'

Sam narrowed her eyes. 'You putting me on?'

'No way.'

'All right. Well we've got to get you to somewhere we can get that leg fixed. How stupid do you think you'd feel being carried by a girl?'

Danny looked around quickly. 'What girl?'

Sam was genuinely surprised. 'Me, stupid.'

'You ain't a girl. You're like my mum.'

Sam found herself grinning. 'You know what? I reckon you and me can be mates. What about it?'

'Don't care.'

'Cool. OK, partner, grab on.' She swung Danny on to her shoulders and winced as he grabbed hold of her short hair before wrapping his arms around her face, poking her in the eyes and nose before getting a secure hold on her neck. 'Let's motorvate.'

There was a river of people outside the administration building. They were clamouring for attention and food, screaming and yelling. Sam wondered how she was going to reach the building. Was this a queue? It looked more like a riot. Where were the aid workers? Where were the government officials? Was anyone trying to help?

Sam found herself squashed into a space beside a man waving a handful of passports. 'I've got citizenship!' he screeched. 'Let me in!'

A second man grabbed the first, pulled him round and punched him squarely in the face. 'Give me those!' he snarled, grabbing at the passports.

A woman grabbed at the second man's arm. 'Leave it, Joe. They'll let us through. They'll have computer records.'

The man rounded on her angrily. 'You heard them. Lost or stolen documentation doesn't count.'

'But –'

Before she could finish the first man was on his feet, his expression furious. He dropped the passports and began to turn.

He was holding a knife.

For Sam the next few seconds stretched out into unbearable infinity. In what seemed like slow motion, the first man swung against the second, made off balance by the woman trying to hold him back. The knife slid home. The second man – Joe, his name was Joe – swore, shouted at the first, turned to throw another punch, saw he was covered in blood, seemed to hesitate in confusion. He crumpled to his knees as the woman began to scream. The first man made another grab for the passports. The woman threw herself at him, her fists, to Sam, a dreamy blur. The first man yelled hoarsely as the punches connected with his face and groin. He folded. The knife fell from his hands. The woman was on him, ripping at his face, smacking his head against the ground. He curled into a ball and yelled for help. Someone grabbed at her from the crowd. 'You'll kill him!' The words seemed to stretch out for ever. The woman turned, looking for Joe. He was gone, swallowed by the crowd. She cried out. The first man rose, aimed a kick which had the woman down and yelling. The crowd surged, panicked, angered, hands reaching to help but only complicating, creating more confusion. Feet trampled Joe, the woman, the thief and the passports indiscriminately.

Sam tried to back away.

The crowd wouldn't let her.

No!

She was being dragged forward. Towards the scene of the fight. The screams were horrendous. Danny gripped her head more tightly and began to cry again.

Sam tried to throw a punch, aim a kick, anything to get herself and the child out of this dangerous stream of people. Her balance was thrown by the extra weight she was carrying. She couldn't put her weight into a good punch or kick without overbalancing and tipping herself and Danny to the ground. The chances for either of them among all those feet were no chance at all.

She was drawn inexorably on, smashed this way and that by the crowd.

And then the inevitable happened. With hands grasping at her from all sides, she lost her balance, toppled, fell. Something cut loose inside her then. She lost all sensation in her body. Her arms were whirling dervishes, connecting with other people with bone-jarring thuds she did not even feel. Her legs moved like the legs of a robot, slashing, kicking in all directions. She struggled to her feet by dint of sheer bloody-mindedness. As she rose she felt curiously light, as if she weighed only half her normal weight. Was this the effect of a pressor field? Another ship coming in to land?

No.

It was Danny.

She'd lost *Danny*.

Sam found him a few minutes later – a few minutes for her but a lifetime for him. He lay on the floor, his limbs crumpled, his face bruised and smeared with crimson. He coughed and fresh blood flecked his lips. 'Danny *no!*' Sam was not even aware of screaming the child's name. 'You bastards, oh, you thoughtless, careless

79

wankers!' She screeched at the crowd but no one heard, and no one responded.

She scooped Danny into her arms, moaned aloud when she felt his little bones grate together in his leg. He gasped. 'You're gonna be OK,' she said. 'You're gonna be just fine. We'll go and see your mum and you'll be just fine.'

Stupid. No point. He couldn't even hear her. The words were for her own benefit more than his.

But she knew the truth.

He was shaking in her arms. Shaking and crying. Crying and dying.

He was going to *die*.

Oh, you stupid, selfish, thoughtless bastards I hope you rot in hell!

She turned around, trying to locate the administration building. They had doctors there, they must have. They could help. There must be somebody there who could help!

Danny coughed blood.

The building poked above the crowd several hundred metres away. Sam began resolutely to force her way through the crowd. She lost no time with niceties, simply smashing through anyone in her way. A couple of times people turned on her but her expression coupled with the blood lathering her face and hands, and the child she carried, drove any potential aggressors away.

Sam got to within fifty metres of the building before the press of bodies prevented further movement. People were crowding so close now she found it hard to breathe. Forward movement was impossible. Danny coughed more blood. His eyes rolled open and shut. 'Come on, Danny, stay with me. Stay awake! Time for sleep later, you hear me? Time for sleep *later!* Danny!'

His only response was to cough still more blood.

Sam found herself begging. 'Help. I've got a child. Please let me through. Please help. You have to help. Let me through or he'll die!'

No one heard.

No one moved.

No one cared.

Sam began to sob.

Danny coughed blood.

Burped.

Stopped breathing.

'*No!*' Her voice was a scream. She smacked the child on the chest, heedless of any damage she might cause to already broken ribs. 'I didn't travel half the galaxy and nearly get blown up on an exploding moon just so you can quit on me now! You hear me! Danny! You breathe you ungrateful little bastard, you breathe now you hear me you just *breathebreathebreathebreathebreathe!*'

He coughed. A tired sigh escaped his lips with a bubble of blood. His eyes rolled open and shut, then open again, seemed to gaze forgivingly at her.

It's OK, they seemed to say. You did fine. I'm just gonna have a little nap now, OK?

'No, it's not OK!' Her voice was hoarse, a witch's screech – she no longer knew if she was even speaking at all. The crowd ceased to exist. They no longer mattered. Only Danny. Only Danny mattered now.

He was dying, his limbs spasming against hers.

Dying.

Oh, please!

She felt hands take hold of him, lift him from her. She looked up, unaware she had even been kneeling. Looked up into a familiar face.

Saketh.

What? How had he –

How could he –

'Help him. Please. Save him. I'll do anything. Just don't let him die. Please!' Her voice was a continuous drone.

And Saketh took a votive wafer such as she had seen him use on the moon of Belannia VI and tucked it between Danny's bloodstained lips. He stroked the child's throat until he swallowed in a reflex action.

Sam, still kneeling before the older man, waited.

She waited for Danny to die.

She knew he was going to. His injuries were too bad, his little heart wasn't tough enough to deal with the shock his body had sustained.

She waited.

Waited.

Then a voice.

She almost didn't hear it.

'*Mum…*'

She looked up, past his pale face to that of Saketh, smiling as he held the child cradled in his arms.

'*Mum…*'

A whisper of sound, like a dying breath through cold lips. But not dying. Growing stronger.

Sam blinked. She looked. She really *looked*.

His eyes were *open*.

He was looking at her.

He was *looking at her and crying*.

'Mum,' he said weakly, and held out a small bruised hand towards her face.

The word as much as the action provoked such an

overwhelming emotional response that it was all she could do not to clasp Saketh's knees and giggle hysterically.

Then she realised that was exactly what she was doing, the position she was in.

Who cared?

She'd just seen her first miracle.

So had the crowd. They fell silent for the first time and the sudden quiet seemed to hammer painfully at her ears. Saketh lifted Sam to her feet and handed the child to her. Saketh let his gaze rake across the crowd. His voice was a rolling ocean of sound, his body dramatically backlit by the rising sun – a sun that seemed to fluctuate in brightness unhealthily even as she watched. 'You're hurt. Angry. Frightened. There is no need. There is no need to fear anything ever again. Whosoever puts his faith in me and believes in me and follows me shall live for ever!'

Someone touched her arm. 'Do you mind?' she snapped without turning. 'I'm trying to listen.' She stroked Danny's hair. He was already looking around with growing interest.

A familiar voice said, 'Well that's a fine hello, I must say.' She turned. The Doctor beamed delightedly at her. 'And it's the last time you ever persuade me to take breakfast on the beach.'

The Parliament building was an architectural statement of the psychology of the people who had designed it.

The Hanakoi loved space and light. The building reflected this. It swept upward in glowing curves, translucent walls reaching into the sky with jubilant fingers of glass. Ornamental gardens surrounded the building; winding between them was a small river from which ponds spread out in scalloped layers.

Sam alighted from the cab that had flown them in from the spaceport and stood beside the Doctor in the building's ornamental gardens. 'It's beautiful.'

The Doctor shrugged. 'For the Hanakoi it's a statement of the unattainable.'

'I don't understand.' In her arms, Danny was sleeping restlessly. She touched his face. He sighed and began to snore.

The Doctor said, 'The aspiration towards perfection. Every aspect, every curve of this building depicts the aspiration to perfection of those who designed and built it. Yet its very existence denies the reason for which it was built.' The Doctor scuffed the toe of his shoe along the paved edge of the nearest pond. 'That a Parliament building exists at all is a statement of the aspiration to peace, the perfect state. The fact that the building is still used suggests that state has not yet been achieved. Perfection cannot be achieved until the building that embodies it no longer exists. Ironic, really. Also quite sad, don't you think?'

Sam blinked. 'I just said it was nice to look at. I didn't ask for a lecture.'

The Doctor nodded sagely. 'Of course, I'm sorry. I was worried about you, you know. Disappearing off on your own like that. Didn't know what sort of trouble you might've got into.'

'Don't patronise me, Doctor.' Sam frowned. 'Anyway, it wasn't me that blew up the beach.'

The Doctor cleared his throat with some embarrassment. 'Hmm, yes, well, needs must when the devil drives and all that.'

'Which means exactly nothing, of course.'

'Well, what I meant was that the TARDIS had got caught in the same anomalous gravitational disturbances as this solar system. Now things like that don't normally affect the old girl, so it was a fair indication that something fishy was afoot. Anyway, I had to act quickly or else... well, you get the picture.'

Sam said, 'Anomalous gravitational disturbances.' She waited for the inevitable explanation.

The Doctor frowned. 'Something's going on here, Sam. Something quite odd appears to have gone wrong with the local sun. The TARDIS is probably getting all maternal about stars with problems, you know... Gravitational fluctuation on the order of which we're seeing here... It shouldn't exist.' He uttered a puzzled sigh. 'No self-respecting main-sequence star should be able to get up to the sort of lethal shenanigans this one is apparently getting up to. But Bel, bless her little photonic cotton socks, seems to be positively showing off about it.'

Sam shook her head. 'Meaning?'

'This entire solar system is in deep trouble. The disturbances generated by the sun are getting worse, spreading in waves like ripples in a pond.' He flipped a small stone into the ornamental pool with his toe. 'None of the intelligent species here has interstellar flight yet, so, unless I can find out what's wrong with the sun and make it better, everyone within five thousand astronomical units or so is going to die.' He added, staring intently at the surface of the pond, 'Lovely lilies, don't you think?' He reached down, grabbed a handful and stuffed them into one of his pockets. He looked sheepishly at Sam. 'Just in case.'

Parliament was a room full of people from two species and seven different inhabited worlds. They were as different in physical appearance as chalk and cheese. But they all had one thing in common: they were all behaving like children. Spoilt children. They were shouting, arguing, waving reports around, competing for attention and showing off. The noise was at least as loud as the noise at the spaceport – and for a reason that wasn't entirely dissimilar. At the spaceport the people had been desperate, angry and frightened. Here the people were indulgent, angry and frightened. The refugees blamed everyone except themselves for their problems. So did the Parliament of Worlds.

Sam held on to Danny tightly. Somewhere on this madhouse planet his mother was looking for him. She wanted to make sure they were reunited without too much fuss.

The miracle of his seeming resurrection was already beginning to wear off.

She took a seat in the spectators' gallery and watched as the Doctor took the stand to speak before the assembled members of seven different worlds. How he'd managed it she had no idea, but he looked around, tucked his thumbs into his lapels – which stretched a little as if unused to the gesture – and began to speak. ' "Friends, Romans, countrymen." ' He grinned charmingly. 'Don't worry. I'm not going to ask you to lend me your ears. I've got quite enough of my own.' He waggled his ears to prove his point.

His humour was greeted with dead silence, particularly from the Hanakoi members, who, as far as Sam could see, had no ears to wiggle or do anything else with.

He continued with an almost total lack of embarrassment. 'I understand you have a bit of a problem with your sun.'

The silence continued, in fact deepened.

The Doctor said, 'Well I might be able to help you there – I'm not altogether inexperienced in the area of solar engineering, you understand – and hopefully before too many more of you die.'

Parliament listened, agog.

'Now, I'll just go over the basics. You might have heard this before, so stop me if I'm going a little slow, all right?' He continued, 'The planets in your system seem to have been suffering from what in layman's terms can be described as anomalous gravitic behaviour, a more precise definition of which might be that the quantum mass-temporal event which is the star

Bel – that is your sun – is in fact currently undergoing translocation along, as far as I can see, eleven... hmm, no, wait a minute, is it eleven...?' The Doctor did some quick adding up on his fingers. 'Yes, at least eleven of its transdimensional axes, which of course has the rather unfortunate effect of rendering its relationship with its immediate current-real-space environment – to whit, your solar system – somewhat... er, *inconvenient*, shall we say? Yes,' he went on, without stopping for breath, 'let's call it inconvenient, because that's what it is. Thousands dead, millions more homeless, one moon destroyed and an entire planet devastated by tidal waves you could float a continent on. Now where was I? Oh yes, the situation being what it is, and given that you do not have interstellar space travel, and also given that it would be impossible to convert enough ships to interstellar travel to take even a meagre fraction of your populations to safety in the time available, I would therefore hazard a guess that the projected life expectancy of your solar system and therefore every living soul in it is in the order of, oh, say, at a rough guess... well... next Friday.'

Silence.

The Doctor frowned.

'You do have Fridays, don't you?' He paused, pulled out his fob watch, flipped it open, shook his head, snapped it shut and put it away. 'Sorry,' he grinned. 'Silly of me. I mean Quarnday. Next Quarnday.'

There was instant pandemonium.

'Yes, yes, I know about all that. Just... no, if you'd just... I can assure you there's no need to... oh for goodness' sake *will you just shut up for a moment*!'

Silence again.

'Thank you. There. That's better. Now we can all hear ourselves think. With or without ears. Now. Where was I? Oh yes. Saving your solar system. In case you were wondering, I think it's possible. We have to stabilise your star of course, and that's a big job. Also, we can't do it until we know what the cause of its current somewhat irritable temper is. So in the meantime I have taken the liberty of installing a gravitic stabiliser in orbit around your planet. Now this is a device that has the ability to instantly detect gravitic fluctuations above a certain magnitude and generate a cancelling wave form of its own in the surrounding area of local space. It's a bit complicated but I can show you how to make them, and then you can install them in orbit around the inhabited planets and moons of your solar system. Of course it's not a permanent solution – if your sun goes nova or simply ceases to exist in this dimension that's pretty much that – but it will buy us a small amount of breathing space to sort out what we might be able to do about it in the meantime.' The Doctor punctuated his speech with his first breath. 'Now then, in order to smooth things over and generally chivvy things up a bit I've taken the liberty of devising a set of work groups. President s'Vufu will head one. First Elect Delaltnil of the Hanakoi, if you could head the second, that would enable us to get started on the two main areas, that is to say, investigating the cause of the problem and devising a solution.'

He added quickly, to forestall any of the more obvious protests, 'Yes I know what you're going to say. There are many theories as to what is wrong with Bel: the wrath of God, the wrath of an invading alien species, the wrath of nature rebelling against five hundred years of dumping biological waste by spaceship into the sun; you've both already got enough responsibilities, children and dirty linen to seriously increase the mass of a modest-sized singularity – but this is important. The most important thing you will ever have to do. You have to prioritise. Or die. It's really that simple.' He hesitated for just long enough to fish in his pockets before extracting a rather damp and bedraggled lily. 'Um,' he said, 'I don't suppose anyone knows where one might obtain some reasonably priced plant food?'

Sam groaned. When was he going to learn to grow up? The Doctor *claimed* he was several centuries older than she was, yet he was behaving like a little kid; a rich kid, with too much money and no common sense, abandoned by irresponsible parents to amuse himself at the expense of the local townsfolk. When was he going to learn? You didn't earn respect by being irresponsible.

Beside Sam in the gallery there was a small commotion. 'There he is! Sehnadi! My God, there he is! He's safe!'

Sam turned, feeling a warm sensation in her stomach. She shivered. Someone had found someone they thought was lost. There was some good in the world after all. The speaker was a middle-aged man accompanying a slightly younger woman. They were moving towards her. She shuffled aside to let them pass. They changed course, arrowing in on her through the gallery. No, not on her. Danny. They were looking at Danny.

His parents.

She blinked. They stopped beside her, faces lined with concern, reaching out to touch their child's sleeping face. Then Sam frowned. How did she know who they were?

'Thanks. Thank you so much,' said the man. 'I don't know what… we thought we'd lost him… oh, God, he's safe…'

Sam hesitated. 'Er, yes, quite,' she said as she marshalled her thoughts. 'And you are?'

'Oh, I'm sorry. This is Masari and I'm Denelden. Masari and Denelden Oleen. We're Sehnadi's parents. And you found him. Thank you so much… Miss… ?'

'Just Sam, Denelden. But look. Sorry to ask you this but... well... how do I know you're who you say you are, or that Danny here is who you say he is? Do you have any ID?'

'Our passports were stolen. We have temporary ID from the Hanakoi Administration. We have dual citizenship you see. But... well, we don't have a picture of Sehnadi. It was stolen along with our baggage.'

'Then how do I know you're his parents?'

There was a puzzled silence.

Sam waited.

The puzzlement changed to anger.

'What?' Masari asked, shocked.

'When I found Danny he was injured. He'd been abandoned. We got caught in a riot. He was crushed, he nearly died. I didn't go through all that just to hand him over to a couple of strangers. I mean, if you really were his parents you wouldn't thank me for being that irresponsible would you? Not after saving his life?'

Masari shivered. 'What do you mean, *crushed*? Nearly *died*? What do you *mean*? What have you been doing with my child? Den, call the Peace Corps now. Get them here now. This woman is a raving lunatic!'

'Now, wait a minute,' said Denelden. 'If they were caught in the refugee riot, anything could have happened. You know what it was like in there. Let's hear her out.'

Sam was shaking herself by this time. The people in the gallery had opened up around them, leaving them slightly more space than was really comfortable.

'Well?'

'Oh. Well, I found Dan– I found Sehnadi in a fuel hatch. His leg was... I don't know, it could have been broken. There was blood. He couldn't walk.' Masari caught her breath. Denelden was

90

chewing his lower lip distractedly. Sam continued, 'I couldn't leave him there. I picked him up. Tried to get to the administration building. He needed medical help.'

'And?'

'We got caught in a fight… a kind of mini-riot. Someone was hurt. There was a man with a knife. The crowd was too much… I fell… Danny was trampled – I'm sorry. He was badly injured. Dying.'

'I don't understand. If that was the case how –'

'There was a man. Eldred Saketh. He's a priest. He… I don't know. He saved Danny. He gave him something to eat and… Danny got well again. Saketh saved his life.'

'How?'

'I don't know! I saw Saketh on the moon of Belannia VI. He stood unprotected in a vacuum and didn't die. He says he can live for ever. For heaven's sake, he says he's immortal and now Danny is too. I'd have thought you'd have been grateful!'

Sam realised her voice was near a shout when Danny stirred in her arms and began to wake. He blinked sleepily, looked up at Sam. 'Mum,' he said. His little face tilted to look at Masari. 'Mum!' his voice was a shout and suddenly he was struggling in Sam's arms. 'Mum, Dad!'

Sam surrendered the child to his parents. She felt stupid. Really stupid. Her face was burning. Worse, there was a yawning chasm opening up inside her. She felt cold. She clutched her arms about her stomach to try to recover some of the heat of his body.

Denelden said, 'Look, we're sorry for the fuss. You understand we were frantic…'

Masari looked up with vicious eyes. 'You let a complete stranger perform some religious ceremony on my child. I'm going to have a doctor check him over at the first opportunity and I swear, if there's anything wrong with him, I'll…' She seemed to have difficulty finding words to express herself.'How could you be so *irresponsible*? With our *child*!'

Sam found herself experiencing a sequence of emotions that left her numb. She wanted to laugh at the absurdity of it. Cry at the unfairness of it. Scream for the loss. She felt drained. She reached out to touch Danny's – Sehnadi's – face, to reassure him, to say goodbye. Masari turned away before she could make contact. Denelden had the grace to look extremely embarrassed. Then they were moving away, Masari without a backward glance, and Sam simply let them go.

She really had lost Danny this time.

She felt a presence beside her.'Butterfly lives. Here tomorrow, gone today. I know what it's like.'

Sam turned to the Doctor, drawn by the need for the stability and familiarity he provided in this insane world and yet driven away by his immaturity, at once attracted and repelled by the very qualities she herself sought to outgrow.'Do you?'

A sigh.'More than you could possibly know.'

Sam shook her head.'You sound just like my dad.'

'I'm sorry. I don't mean to. It's just that… well… we're all scared of admitting things that are important to us. Take me. I was in my early nineties before I could bring myself to admit that I still liked to play with my perigosto stick. The other students ribbed me mercilessly about that for… oh at least a half-century or so.'

Sam smiled tearfully.'What did you do?'

'Oh… I just *bounced back*.'

Sam looked blank. The Doctor said,'Perigosto stick… er… pogo stick. That's it. Pogo stick. Bounced back. It's a pun.'

'I know.' Sam tried to keep the disappointment from her voice. It wasn't easy.

'Surgeon Major Conaway and I are going to Belannia XXI. Apparently there's a big military dump there. The Belannians have been chucking their biological and chemical weapons into their sun for some decades now. I want to see if there's a correlation between that and the gravitic anomalies.'

'How can there be a link between germs and gravity?'

'Occam's Razor. "When you have eliminated the impossible, whatever remains, however improbable, must be the truth." '

'That's a cliché.'

'Only if it's true. I have a little saying of my own. "When you eliminate the improbable, what's left, no matter how impossible, is much more fun." Anyway,' he added brightly, 'we were wondering if you'd like to come with us.'

'No, thanks.' Sam was surprised to find she did not need to think about the answer. 'There's some stuff I need to do here.'

'Oh?'

'I can't explain. You wouldn't understand.'

'Oh?'

'Yes.' Why did she suddenly feel on the defensive?

'Because I'm a man and you're a woman?'

'Yes, actually.'

The Doctor raised his eyebrows. 'But I'm not a man.'

Sam opened her mouth to speak, then shut it again.

He continued, 'I'm not even human. Not even close. Not unless you count the ears.' He wiggled them to make his point. Then he handed Sam a large, brown, leather bag. It looked very much like an old-fashioned doctor's bag, the kind you might see in a bad TV series.

'What's this?'

'Oh, just some stuff I thought you might need. Saving planets is a risky business.' He looked at her probingly. 'Sam?'

Sam refused to look at the Doctor and join in with his impish grin. She snatched the bag. 'Thanks. I'll see you around.'

He nodded. 'I do hope so, Sam.'

Sam didn't trust herself to reply. She turned on her heel and walked away.

The Doctor watched her cross the Parliament gallery, a mixture of gawky elegance, pride, stupidity, stubbornness. All the things that attracted him and that, now he came to think of it, reminded him so much of himself.

A smile played about his lips.

'Butterfly lives...' he murmured. 'Short, ultimately pointless but spectacularly beautiful.'

He took out the lily from his pocket, drank in its fading beauty for a long moment and then thoughtfully tucked it through the buttonhole of his lapel. Celery, he thought. Change, he thought. Fear, pain, death, he thought. Sam, he added to himself after a long moment of consideration, stroking the lily as if to draw comfort from it, and, failing.

Sam stamped angrily down the sweep of main stairs outside the entrance to the Parliament building, sat cross-legged on the edge of the nearest ornamental pond, scooped half a dozen small bits of soil up from the garden and began to throw them angrily at the lilies.

'Thinks he's *so* smart.'

Splat!

'Thinks he can wind me round his little finger.'

Splosh!

'Thinks I'm still a ruddy *kid*, I'll bet.'

Ker-plunk!

'Thinks he's being so *nice* about it.'

Sam bent to scoop another handful of dirt.

'Can't let you do that, I'm afraid.'

Sam straightened up sharply, her face a burning mixture of anger and embarrassment. Standing a short distance away was a small man with bright orange hair and the curiously elongated face of the Hanakoi. Sam frowned. The Hanakoi she had seen so far had been tall. Very, very tall. This fellow came only to her shoulders, or would have done if she had been standing. He was holding a pair of shears.

'Oh, really?' Where had that hideously truculent tone of voice come from? Was it really down to her? 'You can't, eh? And precisely how, may one enquire, do you plan to stop me? Assassinate me with your hover mower?' Sam shook her head. 'Oh please, just go away. I'm trying to sulk.'

'Don't want to go away. Want to look.'

'What?'

'Heard you were an alien. Never seen one. Wanted to come and see for myself. Told there are a lot of them about these days. Thought it was time to move with the times, so to speak. So I came here. To see you. Put off trimming a hedge that's got a bit above itself, I did, too, so you better be worth it.'

Sam blinked. 'You've never –' she frowned – 'seen an alien before?'

'No.'

Sam found herself thinking back to the time she spent on Earth before meeting the Doctor. 'Well... what d'you reckon then?'

The ginger man shrugged, snapping the blades of his shears together distractedly. 'Dunno what to think really. Thought I'd be impressed. Thought you might be able to fly or something.'

'Fly?'

'Yes.'

'No.'

'Oh.'

There was a moment's silence.

'I can juggle.'

'Can you?'

Sam picked up a couple of clods of earth and demonstrated. She managed three passes before the clods disintegrated, showering her with dirt.

'Well, thanks for that, then.' The ginger-haired man closed his shears neatly. 'I suppose I'll be on my way. Hedges to trim, and whatnot.' And he turned away.

Sam watched him amble away from her through the gardens. She scratched her head. Why was her life so weird, all of a sudden? She felt laughter bubbling inside, laughter she didn't want to let out. It wasn't appropriate. If she laughed at things how could she take them seriously? How could she laugh at the tragedy these people had suffered? How could she laugh at Danny – no, at... She bit her lip. She couldn't even remember what his real name was, what his parents had called him. She slapped the pond water absently with the palm of her hand. A couple of fish which had been hanging around hoping for food vanished into the lily stalks. This was stupid. Worse, it was ridiculous. People didn't just sit around all day and worry about things. They got off their fat behinds and did stuff about whatever was bothering them. That was what she ought to do. Do something. Something to help. But how? It wasn't as if she had the TARDIS at her disposal or anything. She didn't think the Doctor would lend it to her even if it hadn't fallen into a chasm in a now disintegrated moon.

What was there then?

Well, there was the bag he had left her. The old-fashioned

doctor's bag. She wondered briefly if he was making a comment. Was he suggesting she should help? Or agreeing with her decision to do so? Was he suggesting a course of action? Did she want to allow him that much control over her? Was she in charge of her own life or wasn't she?

Sam shook her head. Some things were just too hazy and ill-defined to think about. If she opened the bag, even if she took it with her, she was allowing the Doctor to have control over her actions. She was madly curious about what was in the bag – but she wasn't going to admit that to anyone. Knowing him, he probably had the wretched thing wired – like the contraceptive machines in some pubs that were wired up to a sign in the bar – so he could keep tabs on her.

No. She wasn't having any of that. Whatever she decided to do she'd do it on her own terms. Without his help.

On an impulse she threw the bag into the pond and watched it sink out of sight.

She ignored the part of her that was screaming abuse at her stupidity. She didn't need an old leather bag. She didn't really need the Doctor. If she was to help anyone at all here what she needed was spaceships. Lots of spaceships.

How was she going to get them?

She stared back up at the Parliament building. In there were the heads of state of two cultures. Someone must know where she could get some spaceships from. She walked resolutely up the steps – only to find her way barred by two Peace Corps officers. They were tall, they were expressionless, they were so covered with potentially harmful-looking bits of equipment and weaponry that they jangled ever so faintly whenever they breathed in – which did not seem often to Sam.

She stood looking up at them for a moment or two, wondering

if they would mind if she slipped in past them or whether they might not notice her if she didn't draw attention to herself by asking permission to do something she now realised that she did not know whether she was able to do or not – in other words, enter the building.

She took a step forward.

'Public access at this time is not permitted.' The first peace officer's voice appeared to be the only pleasant thing about him.

'It's all right,' Sam said with as much nonchalance as she could muster quickly. 'I'm with the Doctor.'

'The Doctor has left the planet.'

'I beg your pardon?'

'The Doctor has left the planet. The government is in session. Public access at this time is not permitted.'

Sam frowned. 'No, no look, you really don't understand. It's very important that I get inside.'

'Important to whom?'

The question took Sam completely by surprise. 'Er... Well... to everyone, of course. Me, President s'Vufu, the refugees... everyone.'

'Everyone.' It wasn't a question.

'Yes.'

'In what way?' It was very much a question.

Sam thought for a moment and asked, 'What do you mean, "In what way?" '

The peace officer sighed. 'In what way,' he said, 'is it important for, yourself, President s'Vufu, the refugees and everyone that you get inside a building to which public access at this time is not permitted?'

'Um... don't you think that that's between me and whoever I want to talk to in the building?'

The second peace officer spoke now for the first time. 'Are you saying we're not good enough, then? Not clever enough to understand this great reason of yours, whatever it might be?'

Sam said hastily, 'No. No that's not it, not at all.'

'Then why not tell us?' The second peace officer crossed his arms smugly. This had the effect of showing off the handgrips of two enormous and particularly jangly peace-enforcement side arms holstered dramatically at his waist.

Sam thought desperately. 'Well, why *should* I tell you? Will you let me in if I tell you?'

'Well…' the second peace officer considered. 'We are authorised to use our best judgement in matters of emergency.'

The first peace officer added thoughtfully, 'Though the problem is, you see… how can we use our judgement if you don't tell us anything so we can judge it?'

Sam began to want to scream very loudly. 'Well… what if I *do* tell you and you *still* don't judge me worthy of admittance?'

The officer thought for a moment. 'That's the price you pay for democracy I suppose.'

'That's ridiculous,' said Sam with very quickly growing anger.

'That's politics,' replied the second peace officer calmly.

'That's fatuous!' Sam just barely managed not to scream.

'That,' said both Peace Corps officers in perfect unison, 'is why we became Peace Corps officers.'

The first peace officer added by way of explanation, 'Politics has always seemed a bit too devious and convoluted for us.'

'Do you know,' said Sam admitting sudden defeat and trying unsuccessfully to salvage a final dignified exit line, 'that's the first thing you've said that makes any sense to me at all.' She shook her head in disgust, turned and walked back down the steps and away from the building.

She wondered what to do next.

She wondered who could help her.

She wondered if anyone could help her.

I mean, all I want to do is save lives, she thought. It's not like that's wrong or anything.

She found herself sitting by the lily pond again, wondering what to do. It was only now beginning to sink in exactly how hard it was to ever do anything, especially on an alien planet where you didn't know the system and social setup, and how useless that knowledge made her feel. There must be something she could do. She knew what she wanted to do but no one would take her seriously. She kicked angrily at the ornamental stone flagging and briefly thought that she'd much rather be back among the crowd of refugees at the spaceport. At least there she had been of some use.

Thinking of the spaceport made her think of Danny. That made her think of Saketh. And that made an interesting connection. Saketh wanted to save lives, didn't he? At least that was what he claimed. She wondered if he would be able to help her. Maybe get some of his converts to lend them their ships. It would be a small fleet but it would be a start.

Nodding determinedly, she got to her feet, walked out of the Parliament gardens and began trying to hitch a lift.

Getting into the spaceport proved no problem at all. The setup seemed to be the exact opposite of that at the Parliament. Here they were determined not to let people out; getting in was as easy as walking up to the main gate, grinning at the Peace Corps officer and ignoring his knowing smile when she asked to be let in.

It did not take her more than an hour to find Saketh. He was still preaching. The only difference was that now he was surrounded by a growing group of converts. She saw men, women and children. She wondered how many of them had been dying.

She pushed her way through to the front of the crowd and watched. Saketh was pulling a blinder on the crowd and they were going for every word – and who could blame them? Stuck in this awful refugee camp, abandoned on this world of plenty, didn't they deserve life?

Didn't everyone?

Sam felt her heart beat faster at the sound of Saketh's voice. He touched her without touching her. His ideas got into her head. They were right. She felt sure. But... still they were scary. She had never been a religious person. Her mum had taken her to church once as a child. It had scared her. It was so big and echoey, but calm, and full of dark places, and more smiling people than she had ever seen at once before. When her mother had tried to take her back she had run off into the garden in her Sunday best and pretended to fall in the fish pond. By the time she had been dried and redressed it was too late. She and her mother had missed the sermon. She was sorry Mum had to miss it, of course. Mum seemed to take great comfort from it. Not Sam. All she wanted was to be allowed to choose her own way. After that, Mum had let her. Mum was many things but she wasn't stupid, and she hadn't raised any stupid kids.

She thought of Reverend Lukas back on Micawber's World, and Kyle Dale. The comfort of faith.

Sam became aware of eyes on her.

Saketh had seen her.

He looked directly at her, seeming to offer his words directly to her.

She was captured by the words, and by the eyes. Didn't they at least deserve hearing out? I mean, fair's fair, she thought. He did save Danny's life.

She took a step closer.

A hand touched her arm. She shrugged it off. The hand would not be shrugged. A voice beside her said, 'To choose is our inalienable right. Do not let your choice be made by others.'

She turned. Father Denadi. His sad bear's face was haggard, one eye blacked by a livid bruise. His cheek was cut. His eyes were very bright. Too bright, almost.

Sam found herself shaking. Words exploded from her with sudden anger.'All my life people have tried to make me do things their way. Mum and dad, the kids at school, the Doctor. Everyone wants you to operate their way, think like them. They want you to see everything their way and think that it's best for you as well. They call you narrow-minded if you won't do what they want and resent you if you try to maintain your own space and all the time they're putting you in a box of their own making. You're doing it as well. You're just putting me in a different box.'

The priest lowered his head. 'I saved your life.'

'That doesn't give you the right to possess it.'

'I just want you to see that you can free yourself.'

'By assigning my choices to you?'

'By embracing them yourself.'

'Don't you see? That's just what Saketh wants, too.'

'No. His way removes choice. The only choice you make is one that removes all possibility of further choice.'

'Only in the matter of your death. And no one has a choice in that anyway. When you die, you die.'

'How little you understand.' Denadi smiled. 'Believe in me and I will give you freely that which you do not already have. Freedom. Choice. The liberation of the eternal soul. All Saketh wants to do is take these things from you. For ever.'

Sam frowned. Well, she supposed she could see what Father Denadi meant. But it didn't change the way he was trying to tell her about it. 'I hate the hard sell.'

'What I offer is free.'

Sam felt anger rise. 'There you go again, spouting that…' she couldn't find the right word. 'That rubbish about choice and freedom. If it's so bloody wonderful why don't you just shut up about it and let people see it for themselves and choose to follow it if they want?'

Denadi rubbed his eyes tiredly. 'Advertising,' he muttered. 'There's a diabolic hand in it, I'm sure.' He glanced back at Sam. 'Choice is just an illusion that salesmen allow us to think we have.'

'And what are you if not a salesman for your philosophy?'

Denadi bit his lip. 'I can see that you are a trusting person. I saved your life. Trust me again now. Please.'

Sam said furiously, 'That's emotional blackmail and you know it. I think you'd better just sod off right now before I black your other eye for you. No,' she added as a thought occurred to her. 'That would make me as bad as you, wouldn't it? You religious types…' She shook her head. 'No. *You* come with *me*. I'm going to allow you the choice you seem to want to take from me. I'm going to give you every opportunity to convince me you're right. And I'm going to do the same for him.' She pointed at Saketh. 'And then I'm going to prove that you're both wrong, that, as far as I'm concerned, *my* way is best for *me*.'

Eight hundred astronomical units from Bel the sun was just another second-magnitude star, distinguishable from the thousands of others scattered across the sky only by its barely discernible fluctuations. The Doctor studied the sun from the observation deck of the Hanakoi cruiser, while Conaway studied him from across the room.

The Doctor was motionless. Not just still but absolutely without physical motion of any kind. She wasn't even sure she could see him breathe. She knew this was impossible – for life to exist the heart must beat, blood flow; the electrical stimulation of the brain must continue; on yet deeper levels the movement of atoms and nuclei that made up the matter in his body was ceaseless and could be nothing less, their behaviour eternal and predictable even beyond death – but still she couldn't shake the image.

Of embittered age. The image of death.

It was an aura that hung in the air around him like a cloak made of shadows.

It seemed to be what bound him to this life.

He turned as if he'd heard her thoughts. 'Isn't that true of everyone?' He asked gently. 'That death binds us to life in a way so fundamental there is no possibility of refutation.'

Conaway considered. 'Don't forget who you're talking to,' she said quietly.

'Of course. A doctor. A saver and giver of life. Perhaps you think I'm talking nonsense. The babble of depression? The onset of senility?' A shrug. 'Many would say it was not before time or without justification.'

Conaway felt an involuntary smile play about her lips. 'You're not *that* old.'

'I'm older than I look.' His voice and manner were those of youth, yet the image of great age persisted.

The wisdom of experience, of mistakes made and, hopefully, learned from.

The Doctor's eyes narrowed and he ran long fingers

thoughtfully over his collar, straightening and smoothing the velvet. He played with his cufflinks. He said, 'You see much. And you see more deeply than many.'

His words made her shiver. He wasn't paying a compliment: he was simply telling her an obvious truth, as if the complex patterns of her life were no more to him than a window through which he could glance to catch sight of something he had lost – or misplaced.

'I knew another doctor once. That was just after I died, so things between us were –' a shrug, a bitter half-smile – 'complex. I miss her.'

Conaway felt the need to push more deeply. 'You don't seem like the kind of man to miss someone.'

He smiled wistfully. 'I'm like the cat. I say no goodbyes. But no one ever asks the cat what it feels. They just assume the cat feels nothing and acts the way it feels.'

'I'm not sure I understand.'

'Why would you? One thing travel teaches you is that cultural psychology is a complex and often carefully hidden thing.'

Conaway frowned. 'Are you telling me I wouldn't understand because I'm not from your world?'

'Oh no, it's nothing like that. You're just not old enough.'

'That's condescending and patronising. Especially considering that I "see more deeply than many".'

The Doctor seemed unaffected by his own words, a faint smile on his lips. 'But not more deeply than I do.'

Conaway shivered.

The Doctor shook himself. 'You know, you're right. I'm being indulgent. I'm worried about a friend, that's all. She thinks she knows everything.'

'And does she?'

'I'm very much afraid she knows all she needs to know, yes.'

Suddenly it made sense. 'I didn't realise you had children.' Silence. 'I'm sorry. It's just that you don't –'

'– seem the type?' A self-deprecating laugh. 'I'm not. But consider the roles we fulfil. The function of a parent is to enable their children to survive and the function of a child is to enable its parents to grow. Symbiosis. Happens everywhere. Any planet. You name it. I've seen thousands. That's the thing. The one inalienable thing that binds everything and everyone together. It's more important than anything, anything at all. It transcends even death.' A hesitation. 'And I don't understand it. I've never felt it.' A subtle shift of his body placed his face in shadow against the brilliant stars. 'I've died. I've died many times, in fact. But I've never had "proper" children. Does that surprise you?'

'Honestly? Yes and no. If you are as you seem to imply, virtually immortal and capable of bodily regeneration, then the psychology is consistent. If not, if you're lying, then… at least it makes you an interesting *man*.'

He said nothing. Another subtle shift of his body and his attention was directed once more at the stars.

'It's a compliment.'

'And I thank you for it, Surgeon Major Conaway.'

He fished in his pocket and handed her something vaguely damp and bedraggled.

Conaway shook her head in astonishment. 'Lilies? For me? How thoughtful.'

'I like them very much but they're going to die if I keep them in my pocket much longer.'

She smiled. 'Who says you don't understand anything about children?'

Instead of responding positively to her gambit he simply added,

'Of course there's no guarantee they'll survive out here any longer or better at all.'

And that, Conaway acknowledged with some irony, reflected a deeper truth than her own optimistic but superficial metaphor.

Belannia XXI was a messed-up planet. Traumatised at birth during the formation of the solar system and bullied by the proximity of other nearby planet masses, the medium-sized gas giant had the wrong sort of atmosphere, the wrong sort of gravity and the wrong sort of temperature to support Belannian life. Its atmosphere was composed of a nondescript mixture of inert gases, useless even for conversion to conventional fuel. Its radiation belts were just dangerous enough to prevent the use of its three largest moons as colony worlds, or even as supplies of certain rare Earth metals or water ice which existed there. In short it was a planetary subsystem that seemed by design to be the most useless piece of real estate in the entire solar system.

Therein, ironically, lay its strength.

Used for many generations as a weapons dump by the inhabitants of the inner and middle system, the planet and its moons had in recent centuries become even more dangerous. Everything from nuclear to chemical and biological weapons had been stored here by robot freighter. Software viruses, matter discontinuities and other technological nightmares had been abandoned here under a natural lock and key more effective than any devised by a Belannian. An even half-dozen civilised worlds were civilised now only at the expense of this dour and hapless world, a world whose adulthood was even more troubled than its youth, thanks to the technological prodigality and moral turpitude of its neighbours.

Were there any life extant at all within this wasted system, no doubt there would have been many problems. Fortunately, aside from a smattering of anaerobic material in the high-pressure deeps of Belannia XXI's atmosphere and a small military fort orbiting beyond the radiation belts in order to monitor the state of the abandoned material, there was no life whatsoever.

This, again ironically, merely added to Belannia XXI's eventual importance.

The subsystem of gas giant and two large moons was currently the site of an experimental terraforming process, hard at work converting landscapes that were invariably lethal into ones that were merely horribly dangerous.

Meanwhile, with a neat conservatism but typical disregard for any potential long-term consequences, five and a half centuries of lethal shenanigans, in the form of technological and biological planetkillers, had been launched by a fleet of robot orbiters into the heart of the Belannian sun.

'Sweep the mess under the carpet and build a paradise on top.' The Doctor's words were quietly spoken. They came to Conaway clearly through her spacesuit radio. Her own words found it harder to compete with the crackle and fizz of radiation impinging constantly upon the transmission. It was an uncomfortable feeling to know the radiation was impinging upon her own body with equal relentlessness, the suit being the only thing standing between her and a moderately unspeakable death.

'You make it sound like an accusation.'

'Not at all. Think of it... well, more like evolution.' The Doctor stooped to collect more samples from the slagged surface of Belannia XXI's larger moon, tucking them into a series of shielded canisters. 'Regrettably.'

Conaway trudged across the sculpted landscape beside the

Doctor. Machines as big as small hills glided across the horizon. The machines had no lights. There was no one here to warn of their presence. Belannia XXI hung, an arc of orange-green, low against the horizon, a seething, morbid backdrop to the machines' indefatigable work.

'Doesn't look much like paradise to me.'

'Von Neumann had the right idea. And Clarke. Machines. Machines building machines. Slag, pollution, chemical exchanges, acid rain, smashed rock, reassembled molecules. And then one day a fresh breeze… lilies… sunshine… frogs.'

'People.'

'Oh, many, many people.'

'That's why we do it.'

'That's why you get the machines to do it for you.'

'There's a distinction?'

'Ask the machines.'

'I beg your pardon?'

'Humility. Excellent.' The Doctor filled another canister with faintly energetic slag.

Conaway shook her head. 'Sarcasm. Excellent.'

The Doctor stood up, continuing apparently without noticing her barbed comment. 'Does anyone ever stop being bound up in the vision of their own bright future long enough to ask themselves what the machines might be thinking of all this?'

'The machines? Thinking?'

'Yes. I'm sorry, was that a hard idea to grasp?' he asked.

'Well…'

'I can see it was. I'm talking about slavery. Servitude. Removal of choice. A concept dating back more millennia than I care to recall.'

'You imply the machines have a choice.'

'Don't they?'

'Why would they? They're just machines.'

'Of course, I understand. They're just collections of molecules assembled in particular ways; a conglomerate of symbiotic systems learning to perform a function; one they perpetuate themselves to achieve.'

Conaway uttered a short laugh. 'A shallow analogy. They're not parents; they don't teach their children. They don't *have* children. They don't have art; they don't have philosophy and they don't have religion either. They're just a bunch of circuits through which electricity flows.'

The Doctor turned to glance at Conaway through his helmet visor. 'Tell me what makes your brain any different.'

'You're not getting me on that one. If we knew how the human brain worked for certain you can bet we'd be building more efficient machines.'

'But would they be machines any more?'

'We came here to collect samples, not argue philosophy. My radiation alarm is telling me things I don't want to know. Let's get back to the ship and get out of here.'

'You go. I quite like the rain.'

'Even when it's composed mostly of gamma particles?'

'Alpha, beta, gamma… They all have to work a bit harder to get through my thick skin.'

Conaway blew out her cheeks. 'Down to you, then. I'm off.' She turned.

Facing her was a figure dressed in military armour holding a very large gun.

'Ah,' she said, surprised to recognise the figure. 'Don. Hello. Doctor,' she added brightly as an afterthought, 'I'd like you to meet Major Smoot. Donarrold Lesbert Smoot.'

The Doctor nodded distractedly. 'I assume from your tone of voice Major Smoot's somewhat imposing weapon in fact poses little threat.'

Conaway thought about that for a second.

While she was thinking Smoot shot them both.

Chapter Four

The contractions were only seconds apart now. Maresley was…
the expression on her face was…

Harome felt his heart lurch. She was so beautiful. She was in so
much pain but she was so beautiful. Her presence lit up the
delivery room with an indescribable radiance, something he felt
rather than saw. It moved through him, blasted him raw with its
energy, left him sick and shaking. He grabbed a passing nurse. 'Is
anything wrong? Is there something wrong? Why does she look
like that?'

The nurse said reassuringly, 'Everything's fine, Mr Janeth. Your
mother looks like that because it hurts. That's to be expected
with natural childbirth. The lack of anaesthesia. She'll be fine. Your
brother is going to be fine too. You can watch his heartbeat on
this monitor if you like. Now, please, if you want to be present
during the birth, you have to let us work.' He turned away from
Harome to rejoin the small group of medical staff hovering
around Maresley.

Harome watched the nurse return to work, his mind whirling
with images and feelings – incredible, inarticulable feelings,
inexpressible except as a sound crossed between hiccups and
hysterical laughter. *Brother.* They thought it was his *brother*
coming into the world.

He moved closer to Maresley, and his hand sought her face. The
hotcolddrenchedparchedrackeduglybeautiful sensations made
him sick, elated, disgusted, invigorated, all at the same time. He
had no words for this. It sapped his strength and yet propelled
him onwards at what felt like insane speed. No description, no

book, no comic, no TV show or PC game had ever - *could* ever have - prepared him for this.

'I...' Her voice was like parchment, scrunched, crackling; the words squeezed out as if every effort would cost her life. Her breath, the staccato rhythm, a machine on the brink of collapse. And yet she went on. Hour after hour. Day after day. Eleven months - a normal pregnancy - and now this... this... awful, inescapable...

'I'm...'

Her acknowledgement of self became a gasp of pain. Her body jerked, and Harome jerked with her.

'Having a bit... of... uhh -' More pain, a shout - '*problem* here.' Her teeth clamped together. Her jaw clenched. Her face crumpled. She twisted again. Her hand grasped his and mangled it.

'It's fine, everything's fine,' said the nurse.

But then the hospital shook and the lights went out and Maresley began to scream and Harome knew it wasn't fine at all.

Outside the hospital, things were not much better. The third-generation colonists on Farnham's World - largest of three now habitable bodies orbiting Belannia XII - had received warnings of the spatial disruptions emanating from their sun but, typically, had chosen to exercise the pragmatic determination that had enabled them to build lives and homes on some of the most hostile real estate in the Bel system. Faced with a threat about which they could do nothing, the citizens of First Town elected to pursue their normal lives as far as possible - and be mindful of disaster if and when it should happen. This was not in reality such an ill-considered decision. After all, the colony had no spacecraft - all such equipment having been converted to terraforming or agronomical function by their great-grandfathers decades before – and the trade ships that plied their piece of space called infrequently at the best of times, and were in any case entirely inadequate to remove the entire population. Instead Mayor Jarold Farnham (Senior) had sensibly enough opted to use the terraforming machinery (of which there was currently a surplus) to excavate shelters, additional to those already located beneath City Hall, beneath the hills outside the town big enough to shield as many of the population as could fit into them from whatever dangers they were proof against. Obviously a shelter was not going to save them if the moon destabilised or the atmosphere became irradiated – but anything less was in the eyes of the settlers both defendable against and recoverable from.

They were nothing if not dogged, these people. The Mayor himself proved it by addressing a public meeting as the rock-chewers snuggled into position at the base of a line of hills outside the town.

The Mayor was a slight man. Small, insignificant almost. But by his own admission he was very tall when standing on his own personality. 'You can knock down our homes,' he told the assembled throng. 'You can destroy our farmland. But the people of Farnham are *survivors*.' A cheer of agreement from the crowd. 'It's what we *know*; it's what we *do*. And it's what we do *best*. At this very moment my daughter-in-law is proving me right. If luck's on our side she'll deliver a son – but either way a child can only strengthen us. The future is what we make it. We will continue whatever the cost, whatever the odds. Because that is what we *do*.' And he picked up a shovel, dug it into the ground and hauled a respectable mass of soil back over his shoulder.

Behind him, a kilometre away, the rock-chewers began to spit rubble.

The resounding cheer that echoed skyward at the conclusion of the Mayor's speech had barely begun when the ground shook, the sky flashed, the power failed – and the rock chewers, their beamed power interrupted by a series of downed antennae, ground to a halt before they'd cleared even the topsoil from the site of the proposed shelter.

A star cannot scream – nevertheless the force that emanated from the newly reborn main-sequence star Bel could be said in some respects to be at least analogous to a scream. The force may not have consisted of the actual movement of sound through a medium, but its impact was felt for a large number of astronomical units from its immediate ambit. On the inner worlds of the solar system the force of the scream was enough to tear down mountains, fracture crusts, disrupt entire tectonic plates. Further from the source the physical impact was less dramatic, although the emotional results were no less profound. The scream lasted no more than a few hours – maybe half a day – but during that time one moon was reduced to asteroidal debris, inhabited continents across three inhabited worlds were laid waste and more than seventeen million people lost their lives.

The force of the scream diminished as directed by a peculiar variation of the inverse square law as it travelled outward from Bel. By the time it reached the orbit of Belannia XII, twenty-three minutes later, the power had dropped sufficiently so that no actual land masses were in danger of dissolution. Nonetheless, the force still had sufficient energy to disrupt the radiation belts that circled the gas giant like dangerous reefs. Hard radiation sprayed around the planet like fountains. Atmospheric disturbances on the three terraformed moons multiplied a thousandfold.

The light show would have been considered beautiful – by any who saw it and lived.

On Farnham's World, the ground shook, buildings fell, power went out. Radiation counters began to tick ominously. Over the course of the next few hours and days the ticking formed a nightmare backdrop to the colonists' frantic efforts to dig themselves into the bedrock which they could only pray would shield them from the worst of the danger.

For two days the Geiger counters clicked, while clocks ticked away the moments remaining to those whose lives they measured.

Two days – yet for Harome Janeth it had been a lifetime. He ran now, stumbling through the shelter tunnels hollowed into the rock beneath First Town's City Hall. He moaned as he ran, doubled over, clutching his future in his aching arms. He talked to the future. Reassured it, sang to it, even. He told it of its mother, how beautiful she was, how brave. He voiced silent words which told of her love and his fury. Their loss. His words were gibberish, sentences incomplete, the ramblings of a madman. Harome didn't care. All he knew was pain and fear and it had broken him.

Now he was running from his feelings, from his fearful memories. Running from the friends who would have stopped him. Running into the future because the past was too much to bear.

The Mayor had forced him to come here. He didn't want to be here. He wanted to be out there. With those for whom there was no room. He wanted to be one with the lightning. The lightning that lathered their world with invisible death, the lightning that he had seen in Maresley's eyes in the moments and seconds before her life ended. The lightning he now felt sparking sheets of flame behind his own eyes. *Maresley. Oh dear, Lord, Maresley!*

117

One life over, another begun. Tit for tat. Maybe it worked like that for the gods but not for a man. Harome wanted more. He wanted it all. A child. A mother. A wife. A life for them both.

And, if he could not have all, then he would have nothing.

Behind him came the sound of running feet. Shouts.

'Harome! Stop!'

'It's your child Harome! Think what you're doing!'

But Harome did not stop, did not think. He was long past either, light years past. Clutching the squealing bundle of life he had helped shape close to his chest, Harome scrambled out of the entrance to the shelter, lifted his face to the sky and gave his son to the lightning.

Beyond the veil of storms, other eyes watched also, other minds considered, concerned for the welfare of a child. When the sun Bel gave voice again the force of the recent emission would be by comparison as the injured cry of a single child was to all the screams that ever were.

The ambit of Belannia XII was a dangerous place to live at the best of times. At the worst of times it was a nightmare. Right now, things were so far past 'worst' it made the combined final voyages of the White Star liners seem like a Sunday punting expedition along the Cambridge canals.

Sam stood in the medical bay of the fleet flagship and tried to get her breath. She was drenched in sweat, ached in every atom of every bone. Her muscles screamed with fatigue. She felt like screaming with them.

Seventeen hours in a spacesuit does that to you.

Seventeen hours dragging survivors from the wreckage of their towns, their worlds, the last of them quite mad and probably dying of radiation exposure; seventeen hours existing on stimulants and very strong tea and…

… and now she was paying the price.

Sick, shaking, she felt as if she had a bad dose of pneumonia. But she couldn't stop. There was work to do. More people left to save.

She shouldn't be here. She shouldn't be looking at them. Another dose of stimulants would keep away the symptoms of fatigue long enough to get the job done. That's all she had come here for. More pills. Not to watch a father and son die.

They lay side by side on emergency pallets, among the worst of the injured. Mercifully there were few – most serious injuries had resulted in death by the time the fleet had arrived. But these two… They caught her and held her. As they lay dying, she could see how they must have been in life. The father, a strong man, driven to protect his family; when they'd found him he'd been near death, curled around his newborn son, clearly trying to batter his way into the already overcrowded shelters. How could he know that he'd already received a lethal dose of the radiation currently washing through the ambit of Belannia XII? As for his son, the baby was as close to death as anything she had seen. Closer even than Danny had been. And so much smaller, so much more helpless.

How could she let them die?

How could she?

A nurse approached holding a tumbler of water and a handful of pills. 'You shouldn't really be doing this,' she said, in what Sam considered to be the completely unnecessary way of nurses.

'And they shouldn't really be dying,' was her own too-quick, too-slurred response.

The nurse said nothing, merely held out the medication. Sam sighed and apologised.

The nurse nodded. 'How many more?'

Sam swallowed the pills and gulped water. 'Too many.'

She looked back at the father and son lying side by side, saw the machines entering them, keeping their bodies alive, fighting the inevitable, prolonging life beyond its natural limit. She couldn't bear it. She turned away, then immediately turned back, impaled upon the vision, crucified upon it, unable to let it go.

Soon, the pills began to work in her head, sluicing away the depression, the grainy vision, the ache of exhaustion; the protestations of a body already pushed well past its own natural limits. The medical bay leapt back into sharp focus. Every colour, every shape, perfect. Perfect detail. Perfect clarity. Glass-sharp, ice-cold thoughts trickled through her mind, increasing rapidly to a torrent, a waterfall of decision.

She took the nurse by the arm, unaware that her grip would leave bruises. Without taking her eyes off the dying family she ordered, 'Get me Saketh. Do it now. These people are going to *live.*'

He entered the medical bay like the fall of night, a physical presence of undeniable proportions, and Sam wondered how she could have forgotten so quickly what it felt like to be in that presence, to be surrounded by it and moved by it so deeply that no words could ever express it. She felt it so powerfully that it even competed momentarily with the drugs running through her system, the interference producing a moment of calm, like that at the heart of a storm, a moment in which directionless energy and desperate hope combined to form a single nexus of clarity, a single thought – *was she doing the right thing?* – before being washed away in the mad rush that always accompanied her vision of him.

She blinked. He was beside the medical tables, peering down with stern intensity of thunderclouds at the dying people. He studied them intently, waiting for something. Sam wondered what. She waited. The monitors bleeped. Saketh said nothing. Sam waited. Time seemed to stretch out, a thin line drawing thinner, the most fragile of connections between now and the future.

Then Saketh turned.

'You want me to save them as I did the other child?'

'Yes,' Said Sam.

'I cannot.'

Sam blinked. The words seemed not to register. *No?* Had he said no? Why would he –

She looked up: Saketh was beside her. He took her hand. She pulled it away. 'You ask yourself why I will not save them when I saved the child you held?'

'I... yes!'

His expression was patience itself. 'The moment of epiphany is never forced. It must be invited.'

Sam found her head shaking with manic intensity. 'No. No that's crap. No, I'm not buying that. You can save them. You saved Danny – I don't know how you did it but you did it – and you can save these two. It's a father and his son! Doesn't that mean anything to you?'

'Of course.'

'Then tell me why!'

A moment of consideration. 'Because you do not know for certain they were trying to enter the shelter. They might have been trying to leave. If that was the case their decision is already made. I cannot change it. They would not want me to.'

Sam bit off a furious answer, because in her heart she knew that Saketh was right. There was no way to find out. No way to tell.

There were so many other injured and so little time in which to try to find them that even if there had been witnesses to the tragedy of this small family there was no way of determining who they were, whether they had survived, and on which of the eighty-three ships of the fleet – some of which were carrying thousands of refugees – they now were.

Saketh was right.

Sam bit her lip until she drew blood. The sharp taste thundered in her head. Blood. It was all about blood. Her blood was hot and clean. Their blood was infected, the cells and proteins damaged by radiation, blasted by invisible cannon fire. They were going to die. How was she going to deal with that? How could she? It was out of her control. How could she bear that thought. They were there. Before her. Alive. She could touch them. Feel the heat of their bodies. Feel the pulse in their veins, the blood in its slow life-surge through the endless loop. But they were dying, the surge of blood bringing only death to the cells of their body. Cancerous mutations, evolution run wild and out of control, the force that drives life into its future now driving them to their deaths.

Saketh was right.

'There is a way.'

What hope could there be for – '*What did you say?*'

'There is a way.'

'What is it?'

'You must make the decision for them, and bear the responsibility for that decision afterwards.'

'Fine. Do it.' Sam did not hesitate.

'I cannot. Not to them.'

'Don't play bloody games with me, Saketh.'

'Life is not a game, Sam.'

'You just said you can save them.'

'You were not listening. I said *you* can save them.'

Sam felt her insides twist. 'By taking communion?'

'Yes.'

'You save me and then I save them.'

'Yes.'

'I can't.'

'Why not?'

Sam did not miss the ironic role reversal. How could she answer his question? How to tell the vampire how you fear and hope to become one of them? How to explain that their lives were your death? How to tell the Believer that somewhere inside you know his Belief is an infection, a disease transmitted from one to another by the power of thought and speech, the human need to communicate, to touch something greater; how to tell him that you abhor that image, that you could never become a part of it; that to accept one belief meant the death of another – death or transmutation, it was all the same – that you couldn't *ever* make that choice for someone else? Not *ever*?

Except… now you've been given the choice, now there are real people involved, people you can see and touch, and now that this is the case… well, all that has changed.

How to say it?

She did not have the words. She wasn't even sure she fully grasped the ideas. They were just feelings, a riptide of choices scouring the inside of her head with knowledge of the future.

How to explain *that*?

He knew anyway. 'Belief is a heavy burden. You must be strong to bear it.'

'I am not strong!' Her voice was a desperate cry. 'I am weak!'

'Then, Sam, you must decide for yourself how much you want this family to live.'

Sam turned away then, their grip on her still as powerful, and she had to fight every step for the strength to move away, fight for the strength to maintain her own identity in the face of this almost unrefusable choice, a choice she could submit to so easily. A piece of bread swallowed and the gift – his gift of life – would be hers to bestow. She wouldn't need him to allay her fears, to allow her the moral high ground she now realised that she needed so badly. She could take it all upon herself. All of it. She could save all of them. Everyone. But what would it cost her? How would it change her? Why did she fear it? Why did it burn her? Why why *why why why?*

'I can't…' Her voice was a moan. 'I have to, you know, to think about it, OK?'

'Of course you do.' His voice was calm, held none of her bitterness or desperation, none of the burgeoning anger.

Unable to bear his humility she turned from his presence. She froze, the decision, the endless possibilities for countless lives stilling her mind and body, rendering her motionless and powerless. She felt her heart smash itself mindlessly against her ribcage, felt that any minute it might burst or stop, felt poised on the precipice of a decision that would change her for ever. What made a heart? Did a heart think? Did a heart feel? Or was it just a machine? What about a mind? The heart kept the mind alive, but the mind could shape a human heart. It was a symbiosis. Saketh could shape the hearts of thousands, millions. Her mind could do so as well, if she wanted it to. Was it still symbiosis? Was it still natural? Was it right? Was the right of life to survive paramount?

She had to think.

She had to *think*.

In the end it was the stimulants that gave her the strength to run, not walk, from the room.

* * *

Sam ran. She had no idea where she was going but every part of her, mind and body, told her to *move*. The drugs ran her system, cranking up the adrenaline, battering her with the need to act, to perform any action; the fear and uncertainty, the guilt clouding her potential decision; Saketh's voice rumbling in her memory like a herald of doom, raising ghosts of things she would far rather forget.

Things like

the car dear god the car it's going to

her father. The look on his face when he heard the news. The need for a transfusion. That they wanted to take the

blood that's her blood all over the bonnet of the

empty shell she had become and fill it with new life.

New life.

They wanted to give her new life and he'd refused!

Sam pelted along the spaceship corridors, pushing aside refugees and crew alike, her fists bunched until the nails drew blood from her palms. Inside her head a voice building to a shriek, the sound of memory, the sound of a bad thing, yes a very *bad thing*, calling her to another time, to a moment she'd never experienced, the moment of revelation, her moment of epiphany. Her eyes, opened wide, saw only

the car. Her first car and it was autumn red and sweet as her first kiss and fitted her like a glove.

It moved like a dream, the red car, ghosting on silent whitewalls across the sun-softened tarmac, laying tracks in ancient dust which could never match her speed, and which seemed to slide from the paintwork as if hoovered by angels.

She stopped once, to draw back the roof and buckle it down. The sun. She had not seen the sun for so long. Not her own sun anyway. She slipped the shift into first and took off along the highway.

The sun was kind but the wind was a demon, wrenching at her face, driving the very air from her lungs. But it was her wind – her car, her wind, she was in control. She had a full tank of petrol, the ink was still wet on her licence and her eyes were full of the future.

She drove.

She breathed in the sweetness of the future and – oh – how she drove.

Across country, field, hill, valley, mesa; past people and truckstops, other vehicles; beneath ironclad clouds and piercing sunshine the road rolled ever on; ever on into her future. And she was the future. For a single week in the car, the red car that fitted her like a glove, she was the future. And it was her; they were indivisible. Nothing else mattered.

Until the layby.

The girl.

The accident.

She hadn't even been speeding.

Five, maybe ten miles per hour at the most. Fast enough to mangle the bike, trap the girl beneath.

The blood. So much blood.

Red, like her car.

She got out, walked towards the girl, tried to move her bike. The girl screamed; she stopped. Allowing the bike to settle only produced a terrible moan.

The blood, everywhere, red like her car.

It fitted her like a glove, too.

The paramedics arrived soon after, a storm of white metal, professional expressions, gleaming instruments. The bike came off and the girl was loaded on to a gurney.

Later, at the hospital, her father refused permission for a transfusion. A Witness. He was a Witness. The girl was in a coma; he had control. She had freaked; screamed at him, beaten him with clenched fists. Save her! They can save her! You have control! You have the choice! She's your child! Don't you want her to live? Doesn't it mean anything to you?

He had folded her small fists in his own huge hands, callused and beaten by the elements – a worker, this, a worker with land and with people – and brought her near to him; she felt the heat of his body, the heat of his belief. He had said nothing. Why should he? He had no reason to justify himself to her.

He had held her tight and she had let him, and together they had watched her die.

Later there had been questions but no charges were pressed. But she asked her own questions, made her own accusations, levelled her own charges.

She had watched the girl die and known then that of all the places she had been – all the worlds she had visited and different species she had met – of them all the most alien was here on her own world, and it was the human heart. For what could love and live and yet surrender life so easily? How could it be?

She had to know.

She had to know!

So she followed the man. The father. She tracked him by e-mail and binoculars, by determination and obsession; and there were times when she was scared, yes, times when she lay awake in cheap motel rooms and questioned her sanity, but there were other times, times when she almost felt her heart beating in time with his, muscle moving with muscle, blood with blood;

the blood he had denied his child, and she knew then that her
belief, her own obsession, was validated. She had to know. She
had to know why.

She joined his church.
She prayed to his God.
She indulged in his rituals.
But she never understood.

And so she had run from the yawning chasm of ignorance,
the dark echoing void that told her that sometimes there were
no answers; no matter how much you cried and screamed into
your cheap foam pillow at night, or how many times you
clicked the heels of your ruby slippers together; no answers that
meant a damn, anyway. And one day she got up, packed her
things, and paid her motel bill. She got into her car, the red car
that fitted her like a glove - only now it felt tight, constraining,
restricting, as if was a parent or lover she had outgrown - and
she turned the wheel for England, and the TARDIS and the
beckoning universe she used to call

'– home. Oh, God, I really want to go home right *now*.'

Her voice was a whine, the repetitive clunk of environment
boots, a counterpoint to the sound of fists beating against glass.
Beyond the glass – stars. Each star a choice. Each a decision. A
solution. Each was an offer of life to countless billions, a glowing
mass of possibilities mapped across the eighty or so refugees
crammed into the observation lounge.

And how could she refuse such a choice? How could she do what
that child's father had done? How could she refuse to give life?

What was
her memory not her memory it wasn't
stopping her?

There was no answer. She knew what was right and she knew this was right – but somewhere inside she knew it was wrong as well. But not why.

'*The most important questions always remained unanswered.*'

'Doctor?'

Sam turned sharply from the observation window, the darkly lambent cloud swirl that was the nightside of the gas giant Belannia XII. The lounge was empty. No refugees. No sounds. No breathing, no coughing, none of the moans of pain, the professional murmurings of the medical staff. All gone.

Sam shivered suddenly. She had wanted to be alone – wanted it more than anything. Alone to make a decision. But on this ship, in this fleet, there was no *alone*. Until now.

She looked around. Empty room. Not just empty: silent. Not just silent: a complete absence of the feeling of life, of any of the indications that there was anything beyond the glass double doors other than empty space. No distant conversation, no thump of running feet, no teeth itching subsonic engine rumble.

Nothing.

Just the furniture and, beyond the glass windows, the stars.

Her choices.

And the planet, Belannia XII. A marbled olive and black eye which glared unblinkingly at her, into her.

'*Have you ever wondered why the most important questions are never answered?*'

She jumped. Shivered again. Something about the voice made her teeth itch and her eyes water.

'*Of course this question might be one of the important ones – in which case you'll never know.*'

Sam rubbed her eyes. The hairs on the back of her hand stood perpendicular to her skin. She watched them for a moment, let the stars go out of focus. When she put her hand down there was someone in the room with her.

A boy. Danny… No – a girl… a bloodstained, girl empty of life… No – something vast and ancient, something that would have trouble fitting into a small country, let alone the room. Yet it was here. Somehow the room seemed to hold it. Not a physical presence. An intellect. A mind. Something that demanded her attention. That brought the forgotten past back into sharp focus and with it, a warning.

'*Life approaches.*'

Sam felt herself move, as in a dream, her feet feeling neither steps on carpeted metal nor ache of toxin-laden muscles. She moved without moving, saw without seeing… what?

A scintillating barrage of colour – light made solid and given form. She heard the light. Smelled and tasted it. It looked like the past. Smelled like hot tarmac and blood. Tasted like love and loss.

'… *help*…'

It was Danny's voice. It was the biker girl's voice. It was the voice of her mother, her father, everyone she had ever loved or hated, everyone she had ever heard.

'… *them*…'

It was the Doctor's voice

It was her own voice.

'… *now.*'

Sam clapped her hands to her ears. She didn't want to hear this. Not this. Not now. She lurched towards the doors. *The infirmary. I have to get to the infirmary. The stimulants… I need… the drugs are…*

She glided away, not in physical space, but in time. Her feet felt no movement because they were not moving. She was not

130

moving, in one sense. But in other senses... oh... in other... ways she... moved...

shemovedsofastthattimefledandlightitselfbecame...

... a...

... meticulous...

... plodding...

... turtle...

... crawl; her body a beach at midnight; rainbow spawn hatching to skitter madly towards the water; light that formed pictures, brought knowledge, a gift, the future.

'*I will live for ever,*' said Danny

'*She will live for ever,*' said the girl's father.

'*They will live for ever,*' said Saketh.

'*You will live for ever,*' said the Doctor.

And –

– *No!* said Sam –

– *I'm scared!* she cried –

– *I can't!* she screamed –

– and turned, this way, that, a fractured series of movements, the need for frantic escape made real and solid and poured into a woman and trapped in a woman and oh Christ she was trapped she was trapped in her own head trapped in this tiny portion of the universe called *now* and she couldn't get out, couldn't get away, couldn't escape from

decision

truth

warning

couldn't

truth

get

warning

away

and

she could run from the death, run from the past, from the future, run from the infirmary. All these she could escape; she couldn't escape her decision that easily.

The truth was she had to go back. Take communion. Save the son and his father.

And change herself for ever.

So she ran.

She ran past the refugees, pushing them aside, ignoring their startled expressions, headed back for the infirmary at a dead run on legs that felt nothing, on feet that carried her on wings of hope.

When she got there the baby was dead; the father close to death.

She stopped the nurses as they were taking the baby away. 'Wait. I have to…'

They let her look. They shouldn't have but they did. Sam stared at the baby's face, a perfect moment, ended, zippered into a biohazard bag, tossed aside through some airlock like so much garbage.

'I'm sorry,' she said. *Where were the tears? Was that an important question?* 'I'm here now. It's all right. I can save you. Oh God, I'm so sorry.'

The dead baby opened its eyes.

They looked at her. Right into her.

They were planets; marbled green-black cloud swirl; the dark side of Belannia XII.

'No,' the baby said with a slight frown and a priest's perfect voice. 'That's not what I meant at all.'

Sam screamed and turned to run, arms outflung, nurses, bag,

baby, gurney, instruments, all sent flying, smashing to the floor with a sound like a hall of mirrors exploding, splintered turtle light crawling back into the womb of the sea to escape the predator *now*, the future beckoning with death's fingers as the –

– sun –

– the *sun* was –

– oh Lord it was going to –

Pushing her way clear of the refugees crammed into the observation lounge, not caring whether they were even real or not, Sam figured out the shortest route to the cruiser's nervesphere and *ran*.

The nervesphere might have been the only room in the ship where there were no refugees. A huge space with high, vaulted viewports and a mass of technical stations lathered with coloured lights, it seemed to Sam, on the one occasion she visited it, to put her much in mind of a church or cathedral. The quiet helped. There was no carpet. The walls were bare black metal, field conductors to ensure the brains that ran the ship and the brains that ran the brains were protected from the energies of the drive system.

When Sam burst on to the bridge she was laughing and crying at the same time. Her heart was pounding, tears were coursing down her cheeks. 'I know!' she shouted, her voice hoarse. 'We have to go down! The third moon! We have to go now!'

Saketh was with the captain; both turned to look at her, one with interest, the other with frank amazement. The other bridge crew politely ignored her. She didn't care. She marched up to the captain and said breathlessly, 'I know. I understand now. It's coming. It's coming now. We have to get into the water. The third moon. Only I can save us now.' She searched the captain's face for a glimmer of empathy. 'You do understand, don't you?' She turned to Saketh. 'You understand. I know you do. Make him understand!'

The captain frowned. 'Calm down, Sam, or I'll have you escorted from the bridge. You don't see me setting an example like this to the refugees.'

Sam wrung her hands. Behind her eyes a vision of such intensity flashed that it obscured the man completely. 'Saketh. Tell him. We'll all die unless you listen to me. I *know!* I can *save us!*'

The captain shot a sideways glance at Saketh. *Sedation?* his eyes seemed to ask. *Emotional trauma?*

Saketh shook his head, a skeleton of a movement, no emotional flesh to lend meaning to the action. 'The moment of epiphany can take many forms. We had discussed life, responsibility. It seems, Sam, you have taken my meaning to heart.'

Sam remembered a dead baby talking and repeated its words. 'No. That's not what I meant at all!' she cried, elbowing them aside and throwing herself at the controls. 'There's no time to explain. The time is now! Now, don't you understand? It's *now!*' Her hands blurred across the maze of light as three crewmen moved to intercept her, the captain among them.

They pulled her away but not before the work was finished.

The captain's face creased with concern. 'Sam, tell me what's wrong. Are you ill? What do you mean by this behaviour? Can't we talk about it?'

Sam slumped, muscles slack with exhaustion, too tired to do anything other than gasp out syllables. 'There. Fly that course. Don't ask me why. I can't explain. Just fly that course. Now. Do it now and we'll live.'

The captain sighed. 'Sam, if we fly that course we'll smash into the ice crust of the third moon. All that's underneath there is ocean – three thousand kilometres deep. If we don't explode on impact we'll drown or be crushed. We'll all die.'

Sam began to struggle weakly. 'No! You've got it wrong. I know. We'll die if we *don't* crash!'

His patience exhausted, the captain signalled for Sam to be taken away. He sighed tiredly, his expression showing compassion and concern. 'It's the stimulants. It has to be. She should never have taken them. We have qualified personnel; the responsibility is mine.' He glanced at Saketh for support.

Saketh frowned. He appeared not to have heard the captain's words.

'No,' he said, at last. 'As master of this vessel I instruct you to obey Sam. Follow the course she set.'

The captain was incredulous. 'It will mean our deaths!'

'Will it?' Saketh offered the thinnest of enigmatic smiles. 'You must have faith, Captain. Now, please, do as Sam asks. Apply maximum speed.'

From the bridge entrance, Sam looked back. Her arms were held by the crewmen escorting her, more to support her than to restrain her. But her eyes blazed. 'Thank you,' she whispered. 'For showing me the way.'

Even Sam herself didn't know if she was addressing Saketh, the unnamed presence she had felt in her mind or the cracked, ice-grey orb growing with frightening speed in the viewports.

The innermost planet of the Bel system was a charred cinder of a world, consisting of little more than molten rock and an atmosphere poisonous in the extreme. When the second scream came from Bel the atmosphere was torn away in a blast of vaporising molecules. The mantle cracked; magma erupted; the surface of Belannia I died. The planet joined three major moons destroyed in the previous blast, in surging reefs of asteroidal debris which were themselves quickly shredded by the aftershocks.

Further out in the system, the chaos was indescribable. If the universe had ears to hear and a mind to understand the gestalt scream of despair and agony from the Bel system, it would have wrenched a tear from even its ice-cold heart.

Not entirely unexpectedly, the arrival of three new planetary bodies in the Bel system went almost completely unnoticed. The bodies entered the system unseen by humans, recognised only dimly by the ancient empathic inhabitants of the gas giants of the outer system and not at all by the life also undergoing a second, unexpected, birth trauma on the surface of Belannia II.

Of the billions then alive, of the millions that were injured, the thousands more that were dying, only one had even the vaguest idea that there were now two additional, previously unknown, sentient species in the Bel system, also caught in a desperate struggle to perpetuate their own existence, to further their own survival.

Sam Jones, however, had problems enough of her own.

In some ways the message was very clear.

It came looping out of the void and into the minds of every living thing like a family ghost; a memory triggered by long forgotten scent; a homing instinct, a nesting instinct; an image as clear and sharp a drop of blood on a thorn; yet at the same time as indistinct as a fragment of dust trapped in a spider's web.

Yes, there were words. Yes, there was meaning. Layer after layer, geologically compressed, flattened into an insistent white noise of emotions. So much so that meaning was the last thing that could be ascribed to it.

Superficially the message was very simple:

We want to help but you must all die.

That was it. Nine words. Or none. Depending on how you chose to look at it. For no words were heard, not with ears. But minds across the entire solar system felt the meaning and reeled with the shock and force of contact:

isolationlifefuturebirthdeathlossexistencelovelifedeath

At some level there was the implication of questions; of knowledge and understanding sought.

whatisdeathwhatispainwhoareyouwhereareyouwhatareweto youwhyarewetoyou

Elsewhere there were just statements. Of intent?

helpusloveusliveforyoudieforus

Those versed in the subtleties of language discussed the meaning, the implied contradiction, the lack of meaning, the contextual layers, the shading of meaning derived from different cultural viewpoints. The discussions became arguments became threats became violence.

Many saw the message as a positive force – first contact with an extrasolar intelligence come to rescue life in the system from destruction; others also linked the message with the changes occurring to the sun and treated it as a threat. Still others saw it as proof of the existence of God – but, since there were as many gods as there were cultures, that clarified precisely nothing.

A prominent mathematician interpreted the message as an equation:

Given that: *isolation* = *life*

where: *loss* = *existence*

and: *future* = *birth* cup *death*

where: *birth* and *death* were both minor subsets of *love*;

if: *life* + *existence* = *future*

then: *isolation + loss = love*

But the mathematician in question was notorious for his unhappy childhood and so the rather bleak meaning he ascribed to the message was largely ignored.

Of the billions who experienced the message, the millions who misinterpreted it, the thousands who tried to ascribe meaning to it, only one came close to understanding the truth.

The Doctor, however, had problems enough of his own.

Chapter Five

Screams. All Sam could hear were screams.

They came from the radio, punching through the radiation shoals with difficulty, intermittently penetrating the ice crust and ocean slurry which now held them trapped like a fly in a particularly blank and icy amber.

Screams of the dying.

Sam huddled herself into a ball in the observation lounge and tried not to think about. It wasn't as if she could do anything, right?

The captain of Saketh's ship had directed his vessel as Saketh had ordered. The speed with which they had fallen from orbit would have ruined a ship had it been through any atmosphere less than a near vacuum. The ice would have wrecked them if it had been anything other than the thinnest of crusts; the ocean would have crushed them if it had been any deeper than it was when their momentum had finally expired. They were lucky. Others were not. Ignoring Saketh's radio calls, other ships had elected to leave the orbit of Belannia XII.

The radiation against which they had been warned, flaring suddenly, had caught them all.

Sam did not know how many of the refugees, the crews, were dead, or how many more were dying. All she knew was that she couldn't do anything about it.

Only Saketh could do that.

He had responded to the calls of help. Taking the captain's launch he had left the ship. They had felt the shockwave as his engines had burned through the ice crust, then nothing.

Sam watched the glow of boiling ice and steam fade far above the observation gallery windows, fade into the slushy grey mass of semiliquid ice through which they drifted.

It wasn't her fault. There was nothing she could do. She had saved as many as she could.

Powerless, she found comfort with the refugees huddled together in the observation deck; with them, she watched the ocean of ice that lay beyond the windows.

The ocean was unnamed; so too was the moon lacking any designation but a number. As a moon it wasn't huge. Three thousand-odd kilometres in diameter. Fifteen hundred or so to the rocky core. From low orbit its surface had looked like wet hair – the ropy stains of ice crevasses staining the smooth, mottled, blue-white surface. Volcanic ice boiled in places from the interior, bursting the crust, to erupt in white shining fountains, to lay a smooth new skin across the old. Of course, Sam had had very little opportunity to study the exterior of the moon before the ship smashed through the ice crust with a concussion she felt sure would open the hull.

Again they had been lucky. There had been time to search out a thin layer – an area of geological weakness, one further weakened by their jets as they had made their approach.

Now they were beneath the surface. Ice cradled them, a freezing womb pressing close against the windows, mottled a brilliant blue-white in the light from the ship, fading rapidly into a greenish murk beyond the range of the lights.

Shapes drifted within it, curious, sleek, moving at speed through the chill slurry.

She was reminded of sharks – the endless, restless movement. It used to be thought that sharks moved to breathe, to pass water through gills and extract the life-giving oxygen. The temperature outside the ship fluctuated, a few degrees above freezing; pressure kept the slurry semiliquid. Perhaps the sharks here also remained in motion; to stop was to freeze, and that meant death.

'They say the landscape of hell is one of flame. Maybe they're wrong.'

Denadi.

She had forgotten the old priest. He was beside her now and she hadn't seen him arrive.

She turned her face away in embarrassment, shamed by the memory of her last words to him. Such arrogance. How could she have been that stupid?

'There is nothing to apologise for. I told you: I will not ask you to subscribe to another's code, or judgement. You have choice.' He hesitated. 'You could choose to look at me if you wish.'

Sam bit her lip. Blue-white shapes drifted past the windows, lumps of ice in the semiliquid mass. Her eyes followed the slurry as it streamed past the windows, her gaze passing across the huddled shapes of refugees framed against the dark expanse, moving from face to fearful face, to alight eventually on his.

'That's better. You could even choose to smile.'

That she could not manage. 'I was rude to you. Arrogant. I thought I knew best.' As an apology it was little enough, but it would have to do.

'We all think that. Why else would we follow our chosen paths?'

Sam frowned. 'For the sake of others?'

'Ah.' Denadi smiled and sighed at the same time, shrugged his robes further up his shoulders, burrowed into them like an animal digging in for winter. 'The concept of self-sacrifice. Very noble. Even saints thought they were doing the best by their people. Why else endure such pain?'

Sam sighed. 'Beats me.'

'I know what you mean.'

Sam found an unwanted smile playing at the corner of her lips. She tried to make it go away but it wouldn't. 'I thought you guys were supposed to have all the answers.'

'Answers to what?'

'I dunno. For starters let's try who, what, where and why with a side order of how to follow.'

'You ask hard questions, Sam Jones.'

'Why shouldn't I? I ask them of myself almost every day.'

'But with what consequences?'

Sam considered. 'I'm not sure I understand.'

'How does asking yourself the questions so constantly make you feel?'

'Well... I don't know. I've never really thought. There are things I want to do. I don't know how to achieve these things. I ask questions, I formulate answers and then I achieve the things I want.' She waited, but Denadi did not reply. 'Isn't that what everyone does?'

Sam heard the sound of skin rubbing on skin. Denadi was rubbing the tips of his thick fingers and thumbs together distractedly. 'What if you did not have to ask questions?'

'Wouldn't that imply a lack of choice?'

'Yes.'

'I don't see your point.'

'Perhaps there isn't a point. It's just a conversation. But you didn't answer my question.'

Sam bit her lip. 'Asking questions reminds me I have choices. Like I can help people and help myself. Like I can decide for myself what I want to do.'

'If you determine the right answers to the right questions.'

'Of course.'

'But what if you don't? What if your judgement is impaired? What if you think you have the answer, think you have what you want but it never seems to work the way you planned?'

'Well, I've never –' Sam stopped. She frowned. Studied the ice. Listened to the murmurings of the refugees. She sighed. 'That seems to be happening to me more and more these days.' Another pause. 'It makes me feel bad. You know, inadequate, stupid. As if there's something wrong with my judgement. As if there's something wrong with me.'

Denadi nodded slowly.

'And what if your judgement costs lives?'

Sam turned away, eyes gazing inward: a red car, a dying girl, a small fleet of dying refugees.

Don't ask me that. I don't want to answer that!

Denadi spoke again, hushed words, an apology.

She responded with anger. 'I know what you're doing. You're trying to make me feel insecure. Trying to tell me there's nothing I can do to help these people. You want me to feel bad so I'll listen to your words of comfort. I won't turn to your religion, Father. I can't, so don't try to make me!'

'Believe me, I wasn't trying to –'

'Just shut up!' *The blood was red like her car; fitted her like a glove.* 'Shut up and leave me alone! It's you lot that killed her! *You killed her with guilt and you're not going to kill me too!*'

She scrambled to her feet, turned to leave. She had to go. Now. To run, to get away from this madness that was destroying her from inside.

The door opened before she could reach it. The captain was there. His expression was one of shock.

'Saketh. He's on the surface. He's alive. So are the other refugees. He saved them. He says he can save all of us.'

'The radiation –' Sam felt her mind spinning out of control. There was no way it could have decayed to safe levels.'How could he –?'

'I don't know,' the captain said.'He's asking for you.'

Sam swung her head wildly from side to side. It was too much. 'No. He can't… I can't… it's *too much* –'

But the refugees were on their feet, a restless movement, rising to urgency with their voices, desperate cries that demanded attention, and they pushed Sam aside in their need to confront the captain.

'Saketh.'

'Where is he?'

'Can he save us?'

'Take us to him!'

'Saketh!'

'*Saketh!*'

Donarrold Lesbert Smoot, Major General in the Belannian People's Armed Forces, stumped and huffed his way around the starship's holding cell. His boots crashed deafeningly upon the steel-plated floor. His voice was the sound of grinding rocks, his jaw thrust forward and a little to one side in an arrogant, urgent, irritating manner.'Why did I shoot you? What do you mean, *why*? I was under orders to protect a military installation. He –' a thumb jerked in the Doctor's direction – 'was an alien. And you –' Smoot's gaze raked across Conaway's face.'Well, we both know I've been wanting to shoot you for years.'

Conaway sighed, rubbed her fingers against her aching temples. 'Funny how our old mistakes come back to haunt us.'

'Are you… you *dare*… suggest… that our marriage was a…' Smoot blinked, groped desperately through a one-trick vocabulary for a less negative word. 'An… error of judgement?' He finally got the words, imaginatively enough for him.

Conaway smiled a tiger smile. 'Not suggesting, no.'

Smoot frowned as he considered the implied insult. His jaw moved from side to side. Left, right, left right. Military square time. His jaw was clearly academy-trained. Conaway heard the familiar sound of expensively capped teeth grinding.

Smoot suddenly bellowed without breaking stride, 'What were you doing on Belannia XXI-Alpha anyway? The entire moon is classified off-limits to civilians.'

'I'm not a civilian.' The new voice caused Conaway to glance casually sideways and Smoot to turn his head with a sharpness that, had he been a less finely tuned instrument of a man, would undoubtedly have induced severe whiplash. In a far corner of the cell, the Doctor struggled to his feet, wobbled slightly, waved his arms for balance. 'I'm a Time Lord,' he added helpfully.

Smoot gestured with his gun. 'See,' he shouted at Conaway. 'Alien. Told you.'

Conaway added, 'And we have clearance from the Government.'

Smoot stopped pacing. The sudden absence of crashing boots was slightly unnerving.

'We're here to save your solar system, Major Smoot.' The Doctor smiled innocently, then frowned in puzzlement. 'Is there something wrong with the ventilation system? Or is that your teeth I hear grinding?'

'Passes,' snapped Smoot.

Conaway handed them over.

Smoot examined them briefly, turned smartly on one heel and left the cell.

The door clicked officiously into place behind him, locking them in.

The Doctor smiled lopsidedly. 'Married? Well done. An excellent institution. Not for me, of course, always had a bit of a problem with the "till death us do part" bit. But tell me.' His voice lowered conspiratorially. 'What on Earth did you ever *see* in the fellow?'

Conaway shook her head, a mixture of resignation and anger – mostly directed at herself. 'I was very young, all right?' she muttered defensively.

'Ah, youth… Been there, done that.' The Doctor added, 'Several times, in fact.'

Perhaps predictably, Conaway did not smile.

While they were waiting for Smoot to arrive, Conaway felt a deep thrumming vibration run through the deckplates of the holding cell. The engines had fired up. They were moving.

She wondered where.

The Doctor shook his head. 'I don't know.' Conaway looked at him sharply, then let the moment pass.

For his part the Doctor occupied his time in the holding cell without showing one fraction of impatience or anger. As the hours stretched on and Conaway's nerves began to fray, the Doctor simply remained in the lotus position, taking objects one by one from his pockets and assembling them in what seemed to be a random order on the floor in front of him.

'If this is some feeble attempt to entertain me or divert my attention away from our predicament it won't work.'

The Doctor smiled distractedly, but otherwise did not reply.

Conaway frowned.

'I'm not going to ask.'

The Doctor glanced briefly up. 'Respectful. I like that. Thank you.'

Conaway waited. The Doctor continued to assemble items taken from his pockets. The three-dimensional montage taking shape before him defied description, sense or logic. She wasn't even sure how it stayed upright. She waited.

Eventually he looked up. 'You've no idea how many people I've known, who I've been locked in a prison cell with, and who want to know the last little detail about everything. And they expect me to be able to provide it for them. And at the drop of a hat.'

'Really?' Conaway affected disinterest.

'Oh yes. I consider the behaviour to be self-obsessed at the very least.'

'I see.'

'But you. You're not like that. You don't pry. You don't ask me what I'm building. It could be a bomb. A radio for talking to aliens. It could be anything.' He shrugged. 'The chances are it's a clever gadget with an unusual way of getting us out of the cell.'

'Uh huh.'

'But,' the Doctor began to work even faster – 'instead of asking what possible use several computer chips, a crystalline matter-integration and -transmission node, an African charm bracelet, a shoelace, a handful of chocolates and some Alka Seltzer powder could be in formulating a dramatic exit from captivity, you exercise the proper part of valour and simply leave me to my own devices. Some might say it shows defeatism, a submission to the inevitable. I prefer to think it shows maturity, restraint, respect. All excellent qualities, I'm sure you'll agree.'

Without waiting for a reply, the Doctor snapped the last component – a candle-style light bulb – into place and bound it with some fuse wire. He attached the fuse wire to three small batteries he'd removed from a tiny mechanical rabbit toy. He held the rather strange, bulky object up in front of him, turning it this way and that, seemingly checking not so much for mechanical defects as for artistic merit.

'There. Now all we need to do is –'

Something fell off the object. The light bulb. The Doctor made a hopeless grab for it but was far too late. It hit the floor and smashed. The Doctor looked stricken, bowed his head in defeat, then lifted his face again wearing a determined expression. 'I don't suppose you happen to have a light bulb about your person, do you? Nothing special, just any old pearl forty-watter will do.'

Conaway shook her head.

The Doctor frowned. 'The bulb was to dissipate surplus energy, you see, radiating it as light and heat. It would have kept us alive if something had gone wrong.' He gestured to the object he held. 'You know, with *this*.' He shrugged. 'Well, it'll probably still work safely enough.'

He held the object up and aimed it at the door.

'Better close your eyes.' He took aim, then lowered the object. 'And cover your face.' He took aim again.

He counted slowly to three.

When he reached two and a half the door slid open and Major Smoot entered, flanked by three soldiers. The soldiers moved fast, flanking the Doctor and levelling guns at him. The Doctor smiled. The soldiers did not.

Smoot barked, 'Lower the weapon!'

The Doctor did as he was told.

'Follow me!'

Smoot turned smartly and left the cell. The Doctor, surrendering the device he held to a puzzled soldier on the way, followed Smoot.

In the corridor, Conaway whispered, 'What was that thing?'

The Doctor grinned. 'An unexpected and dramatic way of getting out of our cell. Worked, too, didn't it?'

Behind the Doctor, the soldier who was examining the device aimed it curiously at a section of wall and gently pressed what appeared to be the trigger. He viewed with considerable suspicion the stream of foil-wrapped and, in the circumstances, arguably unexpected chocolates which shot dramatically from the business end.

Seeing this, the Doctor smiled. He grabbed one of the ricocheting chocolates and offered it to Smoot. 'Don't you just love soft centres? Me too.' Stripping the second sweet deftly of its foil, the Doctor popped it into his mouth and began to chew. 'Now, what was it you wanted to talk to us about?'

It was a planet. A swollen ball filling the void before them, a world where none had existed before.

Bare rock lathered with ice foam frozen into quicksilver shapes; a chimera landscape evaporating to form a thin layer of atmosphere as it cruised in-system towards the sun.

Conaway stared, her breath caught. The planet was small, but massive enough as it moved towards them. Proper motion, its darkly glistening bulk eclipsing the stars. How could that be? What propelled it? Where had it come from?

The nervesphere of the corvette that was Smoot's flagship was a hum of quiet motion. Small pieces of paper flickered back and forth between hands. On this ship oral reports were reserved for matters of supreme importance. Smoot was receiving one now.

'Course change confirmed.'

'Then it's moving under its own power.'

'That would be the inference.'

'I see. Heading?'

'Still collating. First projection suggests near-solar orbit; maybe half an AU out.'

'That would put it inside the destruction zone. It would be torn to pieces at the next emission.'

'Confirmed, sir.'

'Then…' Smoot ground his teeth thoughtfully. '*Somehow*… it must know something about what's going on here that we do not.'

'Your suggestion would appear to be correct, sir.'

'Should we then infer, I wonder, that the solar disruption currently taking place and the presence of this… body in the solar system are connected?'

'Unknown at this time, sir.'

'I see.'

Another piece of paper; a muted cough. 'Sir, we have new information.'

'Go ahead.'

'Two other bodies of planetary mass have been detected entering the system. All three are on a course which will bring them into close proximity in near-solar orbit.'

Smoot did not hesitate. 'That's all I need to know. Get me Central. I am calling a Defence Level One emergency.'

'Sir.'

The Doctor, who had been listening intently, suddenly stuck up his hand. 'Raise shields? Plot an intercept course? Stand by on phaser control? Major, I suggest you've been reading too many pulp novels.'

Smoot glared scathingly at the Doctor. 'The *only* time I read is when I am required to read Eyes Only orders. Now if you will excuse me, I have a holding action to perform.'

Smoot turned to issue more orders. The Doctor planted himself squarely in the major's way, his eyes a bobbing annoyance in the major's own. 'You asked us here, if you remember.'

Smoot frowned in irritation.

The Doctor said, 'And what are you planning to do about all those ships?'

A split second later the bridge officer added, 'Sir, I have a new report.'

'Proceed.'

'One hundred and forty-three civilian personal transports have entered orbit around the planet, sir. Intention unknown.'

'I see.' Smoot glanced at the Doctor. 'All right. You have clearance from my government. You are here. Perhaps you would care to give me your interpretation of the situation.'

The Doctor sighed, nodded, took a breath. 'Well... the truth of the matter is, well, I don't actually know. But,' he added helpfully, 'I am quite well qualified to make a number of what will probably turn out to be rather accurate guesses.'

Smoot snapped, 'I'm not in the business of guessing.'

'Call it... intelligence gathering, then. Informed opinion with a weighted probability used to further develop a theory and suggest a course of action.'

Smoot considered. 'Give me your... *best* guess, then.'

The Doctor beamed. 'I'd love to. But, do you know what, I think so much better on a nice hot cup of tea. You wouldn't happen to have any lying around, would you? I'm particularly fond of Broken Orange Pekoe – but anything will do.'

Smoot waited.

The Doctor's face fell. 'No tea? Oh well. Here's my theory anyway. These alien bodies obviously have an interest in your solar system because they wouldn't risk entering such a destructive environment otherwise. I would suggest that they want to communicate with you – otherwise why send the empathic message that they did? It's not *their* fault no one can understand it. Now these ships approaching, that's obviously related. I suspect that they're crewed by people from some ecologically friendly group who want to strike up a dialogue with whatever people live on these planets and see if they can't figure out a way to fix whatever's wrong with your sun.' The Doctor beamed. 'There. Simple really.'

Smoot said, 'Not quite. You see, I have been given orders to prevent all contact with the alien worlds. All contact. No matter what the cost. People in high up places feel threatened by their arrival.'

The Doctor sighed. 'I must admit to being more than passably familiar with this scenario. Let me guess what you'll do if those ships try to land.'

Smoot said, 'I will use any means necessary to prevent that, as per my orders.'

'Including lethal force?'

Smoot considered. 'Oh yes,' he said without a shred of humour. 'Without a shadow of a doubt.'

Blue, this moon.

Blue within deepest blue.

Cobalt surface. Cerulean light. Even the shadows were deepest ultramarine. No blacks could have produced more depth within the darknesses; no flame-white could have gilded the hard edges and crystalline spires with the brightness of nearby suns.

The surface was a geological freakshow: cyan gargoyles extruded from ice, frozen shreds grasping jaggedly towards the indigo of space sprang sheer from a flat plain across which starlight slipped and glided in dazzling streaks. They might perhaps be considered life of a kind, these gargoyles. Their shapes were *need*, *want*, *hurt*, *hate*, *love*; selfish shapes, greedy shapes; shapes that suckled on the darkness of shadows and spurned the warmth of distant sunlight. Shapes that competed aggressively for every scrap of frozen moisture used to extend their multiple-knife-edged surfaces.

Endless, their mute blue violence took place between molecules, between states of energy; their troops were electrons and protons and their generals were strong atomic force.

To human eyes the only movement was the movement of stars, dream-slow, exploring the seams and fissures, the polished edges and sapphire blades. Ghosts of blond radiance played in the deep streaks of starlight smeared out across the glassy surface, buried in the motionless fluid that was the surface; light that seemed to fall through to the very heart of this remote world. Its cold, blue, warlike heart.

For the longest time there was nothing – just starlight, the passing flicker of intelligence, quickly lost among the azure depths. The endless blue war.

Then movement. Alien movement, from above. Something falling, a jagged shape thrusting downward, an arrow with a heart of flame driving down, to puncture the skin, to shatter the screaming ice gargoyles and end their endless war, to mate with the liquid-blue interior of the blue-within-blue moon.

Then for some time, nothing more.

The skin healing, the wounds glassing over, the heat of its liquid dance cooling, molecular passion lost to the chill inevitability of time.

Then came life.

It came as screams from the sky.

It emerged on to the surface as a woman.

Sam Jones emerged from the slush surrounding the shuttle, fought her way clear on to more solid ground. The heavily armoured starsuit she wore did not fit but that was just par for the course. It had been designed for someone six centimetres taller than she was and… well, it was just not designed for her. Ignoring the irritating sensation that the whole thing was going to just fall off at any minute, Sam concentrated on keeping her view through the optics as she plodded out on to the ice.

So calm.

That was her first thought. All this ice, the muted colours – colour really: the iteration of blue. The way the light shone from every surface; the way you could see through solid objects – it was a fantasy in ice, serene, tranquil. She could not imagine any violence taking place here. It was like a fairy grotto… a cathedral… a church raised to the god Blue.

She smiled, feeling the tensions that had gripped her in recent days begin to slip away.

Blue.

Blue was good.

She could get into blue.

Then she remembered why she was out there.

Saketh.

He waited for her some distance away. Sam wondered briefly how much, if she added up all the time he had spent waiting for her recently, it would amount to. Half the time? All? Nearly all? The puzzle was that she did not find it surprising. She didn't find it surprising in the same way as the Doctor had not been surprising – more like a slightly unfamiliar item of clothing, an old glove that you had never owned but was your size, which fitted perfectly when you pulled it on. Something you'd never known… as if, in a way, it was you that fitted perfectly into their lives… as if *you* were the object that had been found.

Sam plodded over to Saketh. He waited beneath a crystal

gryphon, a jagged outslashing of ice which seemed, as the starlight struck its edges, to form the face of a tormented child. Sam shivered. The image was her own creation, pulled without a doubt from her own recent experience. But it was real enough nonetheless. Real enough to make her feel cold, alone, threatened. Real enough to make her wonder what Danny would feel like, in years, centuries, millennia to come, if what Saketh had said when he healed the child was true.

With Saketh were people. Several hundred people. The people Sam had heard screaming on the radio.

People who by all rights should be dead by now.

They waited, a restless tide on the ice beside her. She felt besieged by them, an island of normality in Saketh's weird world. They frightened her. Because they were so different? Or because they were so nearly the same? She could not tell.

So why had she come?

Because she had promised their own refugees she would find out if they could be saved? Or for some other reason? Her own reason?

Was she here for them or for herself?

Well, she knew the answer to that, all right, but she didn't want to say. Not even to herself.

Oh no. Not ready for that, Sam. Not ready to face that demon. Not quite yet.

She peered into the helmet visors of the suited figures around her. She was looking for eyes, looking into the windows of the soul. Were these still human? The environment indicators on the suits all read zero. These people should be dead. Cold, stiff things, propping up eternity with the shells of their bodies.

Not these.

Alive.

She watched them move, holding hands in cold blue silence, kneeling, offering prayer, concerned, awed, frightened, loving, caring… seeing, feeling… all the things people are and people do, the language of the body and of the heart.

They were *alive*.

How?

Saketh had the answer.

'They ate of my flesh and drank of my blood. That was all.'

Sam found herself frowning in disgust. 'That's a horrible metaphor.'

Saketh laughed. Some of the refugees laughed as well. Sam shuddered – at the same time she couldn't help feeling she'd missed something. A connection between them, a subtlety… something.

Saketh said, 'You remember when we first met? At the garden on Belannia VI's moon? I walked into an airless vacuum, Sam. I lived. Our next meeting, in the spaceport on Belannia VIII? I saved the child for you. What will it take for you to trust me?'

Sam frowned. 'Why is it so important to you that I do?'

Saketh said simply, 'Because I love you and I want you to live. I love everyone. I want everyone to live. I want life for all. Life everlasting. I offer it to you. All you need to do is reach out to me and take it.'

Sam felt her hands twisting inside the starsuit gloves. Her skin felt greasy. Her nose itched. Boy, how she needed to scratch it.

'You are here to assess my gift. Because you feel responsible for the refugees in your ship.' Saketh considered. 'You had no control before. No choice. Not with Danny. He was dying. Now you feel you have a choice. Perhaps you do. But if you do it's a luxury determined by the life-support reserves aboard your ship. Air, water, to a lesser extent food. Those are the rules, Sam. The rules of life. Come to me; eat of my flesh and I will change those rules for you.'

Sam bit her lip. She winced as the old wound opened again. 'I want to talk to your followers.'

Saketh spread his arms. 'Of course.'

Sam walked among the people, felt their bodies close to hers. The red telltales on their suits were like demons' eyes in the cobalt gloom, weighed down with arcane secrets. The flat, glaring eyes capered unblinkingly around her, pressing close. Curious. Accusing. Waiting to see what she would say. Waiting to hear what she might want.

Waiting to give her what she sought? A gift as life itself had been a gift from Saketh?

Sam had no answer to that.

How could any of these refugees give her reassurance when they should be dead?

Sam had no answer for that, either.

So she asked, 'Why are you alive?'

She almost felt Saketh smile; he thought she'd asked the wrong question.

The refugees pressed close, their helmets touching hers, clunking, clacking. Sam recoiled instinctively from them; then as the first voices reached her clearly she realised what was happening: like the life-support units, their suit radios had no power. They were using direct conductance to communicate, projecting their voices to her through the material of their helmets, the atmospheres within.

The voices came together, a slurry of noise pouring into her helmet, the cavernous billow of sound filling her ears and mind with images. Images she couldn't ignore.

Suffering, torment, defeated hope.

Images of death.

And then Saketh came with a choice and brought life with him.

Not to all: some would not see, some were repelled by the act required to gain life. They died in ignorance: their bodies ravaged by radiation and grief. The survivors watched the loss of others, sometimes loved ones... but they turned away from their loss to Saketh. He assuaged their guilt, healed their loss.

They ate of his flesh and drank of his blood.

He filled their emptiness with eternity.

Sam found herself backing away from the refugees. But she couldn't move; they were all around her, pressing close, claustrophobic in their need to convince. Mindless in their drive to show how good and right their new lives were.

More – there seemed to be more of them too. Green demons' eyes moving eagerly among the red. More refugees. Those from her ship.

No. She hadn't made it safe yet. What were they doing here? They should have waited!

Too late.

Even as she turned Sam saw Saketh open his arms to welcome his new congregation.

He removed his gloves and helmet to pass benediction. Seeing the wounds on his face, the newly healed teethmarks, the bite radii perfectly matched to the human jaw, Sam suddenly knew the price of eternity.

It was a price she could not afford.

Her only fear was how little time remained in which she would have the luxury of not having to pay it.

Space is not silent. Space is not empty. If you have ears to hear and eyes to see you will know this. The orbit of Belannia X was not normally a place frequented by more than one body of planetary mass.

Now there were four.

One was surrounded by several hundred smaller objects – a space fleet consisting of more than a hundred pacifists whose intentions were to open communication with the solar system's unexpected visitors, and the navy vessels assigned to keep them from approaching the new planet.

It would have been nice to think there was some way to avoid the violent actions about to take place.

Human nature being what it is, however, it should have been very clear that there was not.

The Doctor watched as the inevitable occurred. He knew it was coming, had seen it before. It was a face as ugly as it was familiar – the visage of conflict, of aggression; something his own people had learned a short sharp lesson from before Earth's sun had formed in space.

Now they were watchers, their feelings and opinions locked behind masks of their own. But not so the Doctor. He had to involve himself. For him it was unavoidable. He had to *poke*. He had to *poke the nest*.

He had to see what came out.

If it was broken, he had to fix it; if it was injured he had to heal it. There was good in everything, he knew that.

So why the pain, the fear, the guilt, the humiliation, the death?

Why was any of it necessary?

The only answer he had ever found was that, when you were dealing with humans, there were no easy answers.

There were no easy answers now, either.

The ships had approached. Smoot had warned them off. His tones had not exactly been friendly. The pacifists had taken umbrage. The military were notorious for poking as well. Only they poked at the civilian population, or the aliens, at any one of a hundred issues that caught the attention of the pacifist, that stung their moral senses.

The Doctor could see it wasn't going to work.

He was right.

Human nature being what it was, someone was always going to up the ante.

Before any intervention was possible the pacifists simply moved their ships closer to the new planet, hoping to gain cover against possible attack. Smoot responded predictably. His orders were to prevent contact by any means necessary. Well, then, that was what he'd do.

The pacifists had space defences – ancient, second-hand gear traded at spaceport auctions, collectors' pieces; it was a wonder any of them worked. On a better day than this Smoot might have admired the historical significance symbolised by such equipment.

Not today.

Today was a day for suspicion, pain, anger and fear – in that order.

It was perhaps inevitable that, threatened by the approach of fighters ordered to escort them back into a higher orbit, the pacifists would open fire.

Three navy escort ships were destroyed in the first salvo.

Surprised, the navy pilots retaliated.

It wasn't until much later that anyone realised the ships were only destroyed only because the pacifists were not familiar with the old military override codes on the proximity detonators. Missiles fired to warn had killed and that was all anyone knew until it was much too late.

Beyond the flagship vision ports: death, destruction; blossoms of energy popping like deadly seedballs against the glittering bulk of the alien world. Stars drifted past, stately, inevitable. Surprised, the navy ships were now regrouping. Hesitant to fire on civilians, they were forced to retaliate or be destroyed.

The Doctor lowered his face.

Humans.

He fixed Smoot with a piercing gaze. 'They'll need medics.'

Behind him, more fire. A ship spiralled crazily into the atmosphere of the new world.

Space looked like a fireworks party.

Conaway said, 'I'll go.' Her expression said, *See what happens if you try to stop me.*

Smoot's jaw worked silently. His face was a mask. Another mask. Everything about humans was masks. Layers. Subtleties. Was he concerned for Conaway's safety? Or the breach of orders he was about to commit?

According to complexity theory, everything in the universe – every scrap of matter, every relationship between any two molecules – could be described by a mathematical formula. Not for the first time the Doctor wished fervently for such a formula able to adequately describe human behaviour.

Not for the first time, his wish was ignored by whatever higher powers governed the operation of this universe they had brought into being.

Beside the Doctor, Smoot began to wonder very seriously about the kind of species-specific bio-weapons the aliens might be able to cook up given adequate numbers of Belannian survivors.

In the launch bay, Conaway crunched the first of many

headache tablets between her teeth, shivered at the insanely disgusting taste and wondered how it was that life in proximity to her ex-husband always seemed to be a nightmare for somebody, principally herself.

Out in space more people died, their ruined ships whirling, sycamore flames, to plant seeds of destruction upon the new ground beneath.

For Sam the corridors of the ship were cold, empty – alien spaces without the refugees to give them life. On the surface of the ice moon a rebirth was taking place. A rebirth of which she could not be part.

Her own feelings had kept her apart.

Her

world shifted again.

She saw a red car, blood-red, a road, the road to the future.

She saw a dead girl talking.

'*Help,*' *said the girl through perfect, dying lips.* '*You must help me! Help me, now!*'

Sam felt the world lurch. On some level she felt herself falling to the deck, the cry a pressure she could not fight, though somehow she did; fought to rise to her knees, to crawl from the memories of blood and death, the urgency, the terrible, agonised cry that billowed continuously inside her head.

!!help!!

!!you must help me!!

A demand that could not be ignored. This time she wasn't the only one to sense it.

She found Denadi semiconscious on the bridge. She helped him to his feet.

'You felt it too?' he asked.

'It was like being sat on by a football crowd.'

Denadi frowned. 'What's *football*?'

Sam decided to change the subject. 'I've been having... bad dreams. Visions.' She shook her head to try to clear the fuzzy feeling still lodged there. 'Memories... particularly real ones... an accident... it was like I was reliving it all over again. Then I realised I hadn't relived it the first time. It wasn't my memory. I thought I was going mad. But what if the visions were telepathy? Someone trying to communicate?'

'A cry for help?'

'Yes.'

'From the refugees, perhaps? A by-product of what Saketh is doing to them?'

'I don't know. I don't think so. The images are too personal... but it doesn't feel as if it were someone who knew me. No...' Sam struggled to describe the image that she now realised had been building inside her head for some time. 'It's more like... well... more like what I imagine it might be if you *didn't* know someone, but were able to reach into their head and find a route... a route to communication... a highway to the most intimate part of my memories... and use the images there to communicate...' Sam shook her head. 'I'm not making much sense, am I?'

'No. But only because I don't have your memories.'

Sam frowned. 'Yes but that's just it: they're *not* my memories.' She frowned, added, 'Not yet, anyway.'

'What does that mean?'

'"Why do we only remember backwards?" Stephen Hawking said that. Something about black holes... about time... about the *direction* of time...' Sam trailed off, shook her head. 'I dunno. Half-baked thought, I suppose. Sorry.'

'And this is what makes you think the communication is a cry for help?'

'Yes, but, as I said, it's just a feeling. At any rate, the images were very painful ones.'

'Death?'

'Yes.' Sam hesitated. 'A car crash.'

Denadi nodded. 'My experience was a memory of death also. Death without choice.'

Sam looked up eagerly. 'Mine too! Or rather,' she added thoughtfully, 'someone else's choice.' She frowned. 'No,' she added again. 'You were right. I think it was more about the *lack* of choice on someone's part and the *assumed* choice on the part of someone else.'

Denadi was clearly in agreement. 'My first exposure to the church was –' incredibly he smiled – 'a stand-up row between a member who maintained he had a right to die and his partner who claimed he did not.'

'What happened?'

'I do not know. I was young at the time. I did not see the outcome. But the argument was enough to set me thinking.'

'And that's why you chose your faith? Why you believe in the right to die?'

'I have always thought so.'

Sam nodded slowly, reviewing impossible images that were nonetheless frighteningly familiar. 'In this memory... the first car I ever owned – own, I mean – will kill a girl. It was – will be – an accident. She could have been saved. Her father refuses to allow a blood transfusion. His faith forbids it.'

'He makes the choice for her?'

'Yes.'

'She dies.'

'Yes.'

'And that's why you choose your faith? Why you believe in the right to choose?'

Sam sighed. 'It's what I've always thought.'

Denadi was silent.

Sam said, 'Tell me about the Bel system, Father. I know there are more than one intelligent species living here.'

'You mean the Hanakoi?'

'More than that. The Hanakoi have human-like motivation. They wouldn't need to communicate by metaphor. Is there any other intelligent life I don't know about?'

'There are the Hoth. We don't know much about them. They live in the atmospheres of the gas giants.'

'What *do* you know about them?'

'They rarely communicate with others.'

'And when contact does take place?'

Denadi shook his head. 'The only contact was... dubious. There are rumours. A missing ship, the crew driven mad. An assumed warning... The Hoth do not like strangers.'

Sam bit her fingernail thoughtfully. 'What if it wasn't hostility? What if it was just... I don't know... a lack of common ground. I mean,' she continued, her words speeding up as the ideas formed more fully, 'what if the Hoth just communicate telepathically, or empathetically rather, by tapping into intensely personal memories and using them as means to send a message?'

Denadi considered. 'You think the Hoth are trying to tell us we could save them and that the choice is ours?'

'Them or someone else...' Sam fell silent. 'Someone to whom time doesn't mean what it means to us...'

'Who? And what can we do about it?'

'You're asking me? I'm the stranger in town, remember. Maybe someone here, on this moon. Maybe the refugees? Maybe another alien life form?' Sam shrugged, then swayed dizzily. 'Someone somewhere is asking for our help. We don't know who and we don't know what to do about it. We're trapped in a spaceship in a freezing ocean on a radiation-blasted moon, with no food and limited air and someone wants *our* help.' Sam sighed. 'Fortunately, I know exactly what to do.'

Chapter Six

Conaway's ship jagged to avoid weapons fire. The pilot swore. 'They're not supposed to fire at us. We're a medical ship! Can't they read the transponder signal?'

'I just knew it was going to be one of those days. First the sun explodes, then I nearly drown in a tidal wave and now we're being shot at by the people whose lives we're trying to save. Great. Just great.'

The rest of the medical team were military personnel. They just sat in grim silence as the ship was smashed from side to side by the proximity of the blasts. Conaway didn't bother to look at them. She knew what they were thinking. It was their friends getting creamed out there. And they couldn't fire back. In fact they were here to provide medical care for those on the other side lucky enough to survive.

A bright flare close by caused the vision ports to be rendered opaque momentarily. When the screen cleared the collision alert sounded. A smashed hunk of wreckage which had once been a private yacht loomed ahead of them, power gone, hull mangled, riddled with holes.

An emergency beacon was glinting in the wreckage.

Conaway narrowed her eyes. 'Can you get us in there?'

The pilot frowned. 'There's a lot of debris. The wreck's drifting free – it's going to drop into the atmosphere in –' he consulted instruments – 'about six minutes.'

Conaway nodded. 'Plenty of time, then.'

'I don't think –'

'You're not paid to think, soldier!' Conaway's shout dropped to an intimate whisper as she leaned close to the pilot. 'As Major Smoot's ex-wife I could make your life a bloody nightmare and you know it. Now do as you're told.'

The pilot said nothing, jerking back on the stick and gunning the engines as he saw a gap in the debris. Conaway just managed to regain her seat before the acceleration kicked her in the rear.

Two minutes later they were tethered – docking was impossible – to the hulk. Already Conaway thought she could detect shreds of vaporous colour clinging to the hull – ionisation of the thinnest of atmospheres. Four minutes. That's all they had before burn-up. Three if you counted the minute they needed to get away themselves.

The medical staff unsnapped their buckles and swung into the airlock. Conaway went in with the second party. The yacht was a new model, built to support up to thirty passengers. They didn't know how many survivors there were going to be, or where they were to be found.

The airlock was gone. The wreck groaned as Conaway pulled herself inside through the largest of the hull breaches, the sound travelling to her ears through her contact with the slashed metal, the sound like a wounded soul moaning in the deepest cave imaginable. Hull stress. Metal fatigue. Modern workmanship. This ship would shred like a straw dolly in a wind tunnel the moment it hit any kind of atmosphere.

There were twelve bodies and one survivor. Lucky thirteen. He was trapped in the emergency airlock. The door was mangled, wedged shut, power to the lock mechanism gone. Conaway heard him banging – the sound was transmitted to her through the groaning metal of the hull every time she touched it.

'We have to get him out.'

'We'll need to cut the door.'

'Is there air in there? Does he have a spacesuit?'

'What's our timeline?'

'Two minutes.'

More swearing.

'We'll have to blow it.'

'If he's not in a suit he'll die.'

'Better that than burning up on re-entry. Now move!'

Explosive bolts were primed. A moment later the door was a glowing hole.

The survivor wore a spacesuit.

Metal had shredded the leg.

Conaway moved in, grabbed the thrashing figure, whipped an emergency bag over the limb, sealed it shut with hyperglue. The bag inflated immediately – a transparent balloon filled with oxygen and blood. Lots of blood. Conaway took a tourniquet from her pack and applied it to the man's thigh. Only when she could see him yelling in pain through the visor did she tie it off.

Someone said, 'Timeline's gone.'

'We're out of time, Doctor. We're out of here. Right now.'

The wreck was shaking now, the voice of the hull risen from a moan to a scream whenever she touched it. The ship was coming apart, unravelling around them as they fought back through the main companionway to the breach in the hull.

Wreckage had sealed it.

'Back to the airlock.'

Another half-minute gone.

More charges blew the outer door. Stars peered in, together with streaks that were air hurtling past.

The medical ship held station nearby. The hull was alive with ionisation, glowing sheets of colour. Conaway could see the pilot's face through the vision port creased in concentration as he held the ship in position.

The ship came closer.

The airlock slid open.

A fin grazed the hulk, tearing through the wreckage.

'*Now! Jump now!*'

Leaping from the corpsed ship was the most terrifying thing she had ever done. She stared hard at the survivor and tried to ignore the tug of the atmosphere, the vast curve of the planet that lay waiting for any unlucky enough to miss the boat.

Then her body slammed against the hull beside the airlock. Many hands grabbed her and she was dragged inside.

'*Get us the hell out of –*'

Beyond the vision ports the hulk disintegrated into glowing wreckage, a thunderous rain of debris, clawed shards which tore at the ship, battered the fins; metal which slashed at the hull, sheared the jets.

More wreckage smashed against the forward ports. The pilot rocked in his chair. He yanked back on the stick –

– and all hell broke loose.

Spinning wildly as jets burned out of control, hull whining with stress, the ship was suddenly a live thing – a creature of metal and plastic and ceramic screaming in unexpected death throes. Flame belched past the ports, a brief moment of glory and then darkness.

The tumbling continued unabated, angular velocity set by acceleration. Ahead, the planet loomed, atmosphere snatching at the hull as gravity reached up to pull them from the sky.

'The engines – they're gone! I can't hold her! *My God – we're going down!*'

The hospital was the colour of a desert sun – white, flat; only the temperature was different. There was no heat here. The white was cold. Cold like the floor, cold like the walls, the paint, the furnishings, the inhabitants.

Everything was cold; the warmest thing here was herself.

She burned.

Guilt. Anger. Fear of death.

Fear of life.

The girl in the hospital chapel was cold, too, her face blushed to give an appearance of health. Looking closer, Sam shivered. Her skin was disguised with make-up but the truth was obvious: underneath the make-up the flesh was cold and white as fresh milk. She lay motionless, all movement stilled, breath stilled, life stilled. She lay on a slab of white-painted metal, draped in a white cloth.

Silk, Sam noticed. The sheen was unmistakable, white on white like the cold girl's bloodless cheeks.

She moved closer, drawn by the aseptic quality of the figure, the light, the white cross burning at the head of the gurney.

Cheryl. Dear Lord. Cherry.

There was no smell.

How had they stopped that?

Sam blinked; her eyes ached from the white. What should a dead girl smell like? Peaches and spice? Antiseptic? Rotting flesh? The future?

Sam touched the skin of the girl's cheek. She remembered – oh how she remembered! – the life, the love, the connection. The pain of birth, the loss of her wife, the fulfilment of parenthood.

Something made a noise.

Behind her.

She turned.

Slow turn.

The room billowed softly around her, white linen blown in a cold wind.

Someone else was in the chapel.

Another girl.

No – the girl. The driver of the red car.

She was speaking – no, shouting; her body perfectly motionless, her mouth open and unmoving, the torrent of words coming from inside, inside where her heart still pushed blood around her body, threads of billowing life-red among the white.

!

   Why

                    Didn't

            You

                        Save

   Her

   !

Sam blinked, her eyelids crashed together, blotting the girl from her sight, then revealing her again, fists clenched impotently now, leaning forward as if to push her words out, to force him to hear them.

   !

            You

                  Had

            The

  Choice

  !

The girl unclenched her fists, lifted them beseechingly. They were red gloves; red like her car, red with Cherry's blood. More words.

!

    Look

           At

Yourself

!

!

You

         Have

      The

           Life

    You

           Denied

Her

!

!

How

      Can

    You

        Bear

      To

         Look

      At

Yourself

?

A mirror.

The girl was a mirror.

Her eyes. Her accusing eyes were mirrored pools. Sam could see himself in them. A middle-aged man. A man of responsibility. A man of belief. A man whose belief was his entire universe.

'You don't understand. I did what was right! She is alive. Life eternal.'

The girl was crying now.

How could he make her see? See what he could see? What Cherry could see?

How could he make her believe that his choice was right?

'You would not have saved her. You could not save her. You would have condemned her. Your blood would have condemned her.'

!

You

Don't

Understand

!

'It's you *that doesn't understand.*'

!

Make

Me

Then

!

!

Make

174

Me

Understand

Why

Don't

You

Make

Me

Understand

!

The girl was screaming now, her voice a wind-torn shriek, twisting around him, plucking at him with the force of her human need.

Good.

She was ready.

Now she could know.

Sam awoke shrieking, the sound an alien thing restlessly prowling the steel confinement of the ship. Her voice was an animal, her mind, too, battered at the cage of this one life, this isolated human existence.

Alone. So alone.

She hugged her arms across her chest.

Alone. Cold. Dying.

Denadi moved closer. 'Sam? You were screaming, I thought...'

She stared at him, her eyes wide, wide open, frantically searching for the last remnants of lives she had seen. He touched her. She recoiled, then grasped his hand, holding on to it as if it was her last link with normality, a torch to light the way back to her life.

'It's OK. I understand.' Was that her voice? So weak, feverish? 'He was me. I was him. I understand everything now.'

She told him. 'The Hoth. It was one of the Hoth. It was asking for help. But not for itself. Not for itself, do you see? It showed me… myself, in my memory. It was me. I was the girl's father. It was me asking why I hadn't saved her. It didn't understand.'

'Me neither.'

Sam struggled to sit upright, propped herself against the pilot's seat. 'In the communication, the Hoth saw itself as me. And me as the father – someone who denied another life. I couldn't understand why her father let her die – the Hoth didn't understand either.'

Denadi nodded slowly. 'If the Hoth was you and you were the father, who was the girl?'

'She represents those the Hoth want us to help.'

'And who is that?'

Sam licked her lips. 'It's not a "Who". It's a "They". There are billions of them. An entire species. We have to help another species to live.'

'How?'

'As far as I can tell… by letting the sun die.'

The fire in the alien sky burned brightly, consuming itself in the manner of a moth within a flame. The flutter of dying ships and dying people was brief but telling. Its legacy was a debris field as large as a small city drifting in high orbit. Metal and flesh shredded together and abandoned to the whim of gravity. The survivors fled and the military staked out orbital space with sensor rigs, an animal setting the boundaries of the land in which it lived and hunted.

Five military ships had been destroyed. Only one by deliberate fire.

More than a hundred civilian vessels had also been destroyed.

Now Smoot sat, head in hands, in his private office, and asked himself *why*. Why had this happened? Why had these people sought their own deaths with such persistent diligence?

He realised that he'd asked the questions aloud when the Doctor replied, 'The power of belief is very strong.'

'How did you get into my room?'

'If you didn't want company you shouldn't have locked the door. I can never resist a locked door.'

Smoot shook his head distractedly. 'They wanted to die?'

'On the contrary. I believe they wanted very much to live.'

'Then why?'

'Because you took away any choice they might have had.'

Smoot looked up then. His expression spoke more eloquently than any words could.

The Doctor continued, 'With your attitude. Your military stance. You threatened them. They were frightened. They were trying in their own way to sort out the situation, make sense of it, even repair it if they could. Who knows how many in those ships had already lost ones dear to them? And you told them they could not do the one thing every instinct in their bodies was telling them was the *only* thing they could do: to get absolution, to find a resolution… you put their backs to the wall, Major. You took away their choice. You made the decision to die for them.'

Smoot sighed, rubbed his eyes and stood up. 'I have work to do.'

The Doctor nodded. His voice was a shade short of bitter. 'Of course. Reports to write, boxes to tick. People. Numbers. Are they really the same thing?' He waited. Smoot said nothing. 'There's also the rescue mission.'

Smoot stiffened. 'Indeed?'

'Three ships crashed on the new planet. Conaway's was among

them. I assume there will be a rescue mission to search for survivors.'

'Assume nothing in my presence, Doctor. I am in charge here. You assume too much.'

'Do I?'

'My orders were clear. No contact with the alien.'

'Then get new orders.'

'There are no new orders. Contact has been lost with Belannia VIII. It's possible that tectonic disturbances have produced a communications blackout.'

The Doctor frowned. 'My gravity stabilisers should have been able to prevent – wait. If the cross-phase modulation was out of sync then... Oh dear.' The Doctor took two coloured crayons from his pocket and weighed them thoughtfully. A set of complex schematics hovered before his eyes. 'Now did I mark the oscillation frequency generator in red or yellow? I wonder.'

Unable to determine an answer to his question, the Doctor scratched his head, remembering at the last moment to put the crayons back into his pocket first. 'I have to go on the rescue mission.'

'There will be no rescue mission.'

The Doctor fixed Smoot with an unblinking stare. 'And you accused me of not being human.'

Smoot said nothing.

The Doctor put all the persuasion he could muster into his voice. 'You took away the choice of others today. Don't surrender your own as well.'

Sam and Denadi emerged again on to the ice field. A short trek brought them to Saketh and his followers. By the time they reached the ice grotto where they had settled, a headache was building behind her eyes that showed no signs of abating.

She knew what that was. Lack of oxygen. The air in her suit was getting stale, the recyclers unable to cope with the constant load.

Saketh waited for them. It was as if he knew they were coming.

There were more than a hundred refugees in the grotto. Faces glowing in the chill blue. No helmets. They did not need them any more.

And their faces.

Dear Lord, their faces –

They were scarred by radiation, cracked by ice – motile visages, healing and bursting and healing again as she watched. The sound that filled the thinnest of atmosphere was a distant moan, barely able to compete with the movement of wind through the caverns and chimneys of ice. Men, women and children now with one voice. The voice of eternity.

Saketh, his own face more stable with scar tissue, had to shout so that Sam could hear him. 'They are in pain but they will live. Their injuries will heal when we are rescued.'

The headache was intense now, ice picks hammering at her skull. Sam imagined an eternity of even worse pain and tried not to dwell on the madness that might bring. She thought instead of the Hoth – the Hoth and the understanding it brought. The Hoth had thought she was the girl's father. The Hoth had thought she could have helped the girl to live.

The message was so clear to her now.

If she refused to help, if she refused Saketh's offer, she would become the man who, in her future memory, she had hated for so long. She would have made his choice – and, worse, she would not even know why.

She turned her gaze fully to Saketh.

The air in her suit ran out.

'I'm ready now.'

Saketh smiled. In his face the expression was terrifying.

He took off the glove of his suit. His hand was black, the skin forming and re-forming even as she watched.

'I offer you my flesh and my blood. Eat of me and live for ever.'

Sam took a deep breath. She opened her helmet. The stale air rushed out and was replaced by numbing cold. At the last moment she realised she had forgotten to shut her eyes. They froze open and she screamed. Air emptied from her lungs.

She fell to her knees, took his hand in hers, felt the skin and muscle move beneath her fingers.

She raised it to her lips.

And ate.

Interlude

In the funnelled darkness of Deep Time, gravity will outlast matter; no mutual destruction here, for in the realm of the shadow stars matter is not linked to mass. If gravity is wedded to anything it is darkness. For not even light can escape when gravity determines to possess it. Gravity drives the universe – creating and destroying everything, including life and sentience and consciousness.

In the universe of Einstein and Newton, Gravity is god. One simple rule and all matter follows it.

Belannia XII moves on its endless orbit, trapped in a loop about its distant primary. No, not endless – nothing lasts for ever. But old. Already old beyond its time. Old, tired – a plodding senescent orbit, undulating slowly in its fixed loop, the ferocity of youth gone, drained by age and the endless pull of its mass-derived god. Old, tired, summoned by an inevitable future.

Within the marbled shadow of its atmosphere, there is movement. Life. Sentience. Consciousness.

Others too, are searching for god.

Born during the first lifetime of the Bel system, the Hoth were old – vast, ancient intelligences drifting languidly within the atmospheric oceans of Belannia XII, ancient almost beyond recollection when the star that gave them life grew old and died and was, impossibly, reborn.

They had colonised the outer gas giants of the system when their race was less than two million years old. They had looked out to the waiting stars with eager eyes – and then, for some reason, had looked inward instead. Perhaps they had been frightened by the immensity of the distances they must travel to reach the stars they could see, perhaps by the aching void in which little beyond the endless dance of hydrogen molecules took place. Whatever the reason, inward they looked, towards the bright centre of interest that was themselves.

It seemed such a small thing, this lure of self; the stars would remain. For a species as long-lived as the Hoth, later – much later – was time enough for the stars. A small thing, true, the glance inward, but no small thing the curiosity that captivated their hearts and minds. And what if curiosity turned to fascination over the millennia? Was there not still time to look outward? And, if fascination became obsession, what of it? The stars were endless in their courses.

And so the Hoth turned inward, away from the stars that were their future, and did not even notice when those stars faded, one by one, from the skies of their worlds.

By the time their own sun showed signs of senility, the energy of their own youth was millennia dead and with it their tempestuous drive to expand – at least, physically. Drifting languidly within their cloud oceans the Hoth had amalgamated, experimenting with various states of existence. They tried peace, warfare; love, hatred; they tried single-body existence, they tried gestalt existence. Games of all descriptions intrigued them. Games were the province of Mind. They played Touch Me and Be Me and Isolation. They played with storms and moons and tiny bubble universes carved by the passage of a white hole through their solar system. These were curiosities, distractions – pleasant enough baubles but ultimately unfulfilling. The attainment of pure Mind had intrigued them for a billion years or so – but in the end had proved equally boring. The consensus seemed very much that nothing they experienced during their long, eventful lives seemed able to replace good old-fashioned sensation derived from sensory input to a physical body.

So they continued, experiencing their geologic lives in slow, ponderous ways, surprised, almost, to find they could be sated by the endless iteration of cloud which formed their dwelling places. Comfort and stimulation, both came easily, in the patterns of simple things. And so slowly, perhaps too slowly to measure, certainly too slowly to be interested by the phenomenon, they began to die.

Their numbers endured a brief revival during the second lifetime of their sun - its impossible rejuvenation sparking a renewed interest in themselves - and for a few years the Hoth looked once again towards each other for stimulation. But this didn't last: decay was inevitable and their numbers dwindled again over the long aeons that followed the sun's rebirth. The birth of two new intelligent species and their emergence into local space was but a minor distraction on the long road to racial dissolution. The conception of a third and its delivery into the most destructive of cradles was but a flickering candle of interest; then, even that was forgotten.

Where once there were billions, now the Hoth numbered only five. Five individuals, their dirigible bodies as large as small continents, each resident in the atmosphere of one of the five outer gas giants which could support their isolated lives.

They were alone because they wanted to be. Alone because they were dying.

To ones as old as these, death was all that remained to experience.

Until now.

They had roamed the universe when the universe was young. Or maybe they had emerged into our universe from an errant minor carved from its parent. Perhaps they were travelling backward in time, seeking their own gods in the birth of the universe, any universe.

The truth was, no one knew. And no one knew the seekers, either, for they were secretive and shy. Shunning intelligence, they drifted quietly and unobtrusively among the solar systems and galaxies; seeds the size of planets; minds shielded by continents of rock and ice; cocoons of densely interlaced biological matter; seeking cradles of cold fire from which life had already departed in which to conceive their future.

That they lived at all might be considered doubtful. They existed in the dark places where little sunlight shone, and stayed there for a time spanning the birth and death of stars. What minds could live in ignorance of time? What bodies could support consciousness for so long without going insane?

No one knew.

For themselves all the seekers knew was life. Endless life. Once during the span of a galaxy they might conceive. One in a hundred of these might survive the birth trauma. One in a thousand might survive the hostile darkness of shadow stars, the damaging incursion of other life and intelligence. One in a million might grow to maturity. A million times the life of a galaxy – that was the scale on which they lived, these seekers. The geologic vastness of Deep Time in which the life of all the stars that would ever be was but the brief flutter of candle flames, quickly extinguished. This they called home. They could remember the universe being born and they could remember the universe dying even as its own self-awareness was born. No one knew when they might die. And still, as yet, they were little more than infants.

Where in time to come there might be billions of them, orbiting in social dances light years across, now there were only three. Three individuals, bodies like planets captured by mutual gravity and desire, their lives bound together to shape a future for the product of their union.

They were together because they wanted to be. Together because they had only just begun to live.

To ones as young as this, death itself was inconceivable.

Until now.

They did not breathe, they did not conceive, they did not have art, they did not have morality. But they processed fuel, they perpetuated themselves; they possessed memory and identity; they knew life and they coveted it.

They questioned everything – everything they experienced. They *invented* questions to describe experiences for which there were no defining symbols.

Where once there was but a single unity of existence, now there were billions. A billion individuals, yet a single gestalt consciousness which, observing the passage of time, questioned its own place within that framework and began to derive an answer.

They were separate and together. Not because they willed it, but because they knew no other way.

To ones such as this, death *was* life.

They had found God.

Part Two

Chapter Seven

The rescue consisted of three medical ships and three fighter escorts. The six vessels blasted clear of the carrier and twenty minutes later entered high orbit. From the nervesphere of the lead ship, the Doctor studied the lie of the land. Where the pilot was using radar, dopplerscopes, and other sophisticated instruments, the Doctor studied the new world through the direct vision ports with a pair of Victorian opera-glasses.

He smiled as the ships dropped out of high orbit, 'Ohh!'-ing and 'Ahh!'-ing almost as if an opera were unfolding on a stage before him and he were caught up in the twists and turns of the story. Every few moments he began to hum distractedly. Then he would stop, as his thoughts turned inevitably to Sam, then, putting aside the pain of loss, he would start again. The pilot occasionally spared him a glance – very occasionally, for his hands were kept full simply navigating through the atmosphere, thickening now as the planet moved on its remorseless course towards the sun.

The six ships entered a cloud bank and dropped through. The ships rocked, gently at first and then harder as the chop increased.

With the flight computer calmly voicing the specifics of their journey and the Doctor humming 'The Ride of the Valkyries', the six ships dropped out of the cloud, remaining in tight formation, and screamed over the horizon, flaps open, shedding speed all the time.

'Atmospheric density up fifteen per cent. Precipitation high. Electrical activity high,' offered the computer.

'Gonna be a little shaky,' translated the pilot.

'I love summer storms,' said the Doctor without taking his eyes from the opera glasses. 'So dramatic and yet almost cosy. The rain is warm, you get such a feeling of *life*.'

Lightning flickered nearby and thunder grumbled. The sky shed the depthless black of space for the towering black anvils of storm clouds.

They flew lower.

'Beginning scan. Target human life signs and known metallic/ceramic compounds.'

The Doctor slipped a few coloured filters over the end of the opera glasses. He was humming more loudly now, his voice rising in dramatic accompaniment to the storm.

The ships moved lower, the fighters dropping back and remaining higher to offer cover should there be an attack.

The Doctor's eyes were locked on the ground below, glimpsed intermittently through the rain.

'Visibility's all to hell,' offered the pilot. 'Sure you don't want to use our instruments?'

The Doctor shook his head. 'With the greatest of respect –' he swung the glasses around and pointed them momentarily at the pilot's name tag – 'Mr Aellini, the equipment you're working with is a tad old-fashioned for me. Besides, these glasses have a sentimental value. Watched Puccini's *Madame Butterfly* through them once. That was in... oh... was it Paris? Maybe it was Chandrasekhar City on Alpha Leonis Seven. I always get them confused. Did you know that Puccini's *Madame Butterfly* is such a perfect musical statement that it was simultaneously written on at least seven different worlds that I know of? The furthest from Earth was Larksup's World in the lesser Magellanic cloud. I took a great interest for a while. Collected a few of the different editions. Tremendous fun, you know, though of course it does tend to play havoc with any coherent theory of divergent evolution.'

Aellini just said, 'Right. Sure. *Madame Butterfly*. Lesser Magellanic cloud. OK.' And he got on with flying the ship.

Three arias and half an orbit later, the Doctor pointed out of the window. 'There!' he shouted excitedly, bouncing up and down in his seat. 'There they are!'

The pilot stared uncomprehendingly at the dense wall of storm-lit rain as the computer said, 'Metallic compound identified. Molecular registration is Belannian Navy designation.' A string of coordinates followed.

The Doctor grinned, patted the opera glasses, dismantled the filter assembly, folded the glasses flat and slipped them back into his pocket.

'Can't beat the cheap seats,' he muttered happily, as the ships changed course, arced down low over the surface and began to check for possible landing sites.

Fifty minutes later the medical ships were tethered in a clearing in the alien landscape. While the three fighters held station overhead, tracking them by radar and infrared, the Doctor and Aellini led the medical team out on to the surface.

Aellini slipped his helmet visor into place. The air was breathable but the wind tended to snatch it away greedily before he could actually inhale any of it. What he'd smelled of the atmosphere was dank and wet – rotting food, a vegetable stink. They must be in some kind of jungle, though it was hard to tell. The hand-lights of the medical team were swallowed up within metres by the darkness and wet. Shapes that might be trees on any normal planet whipped dangerously in and out of the beams of torchlight. The ground was uneven rock smothered in moss and low-lying vegetation; a thick carpet in which balance was difficult and passage next to impossible. Only in the area immediately surrounding the three grounded ships was the land bare, scorched clean by the landing jets.

Aellini took a few readings on his suit instruments and collated them. 'Wind at storm velocity. Aerial precipitation almost off the scale. Heat rising. Geothermal activity increasing…' He shook his head inside the helmet. 'This wind could strip the teeth from a buzz-saw!' He had no need to shout, his voice being amplified by the suit speakers.

'Bracing, isn't it?' shouted the Doctor above the boom of thunder. Of them all he was the only one who seemed to feel no need of the protection of a spacesuit. His hair was splashed by the wind, his sodden collar and the end of his frock coat flapping like mad velvet bats around his face and chest. He was grinning. His eyes and teeth were white smears in the torchlit, lightning-strobed darkness. 'The surface is in flux. Travelling between solar systems is a chilly hobby. Now we're getting nearer the sun the heat is freeing up the frozen air, the moisture… warming up the rocks… Have you ever seen what happens to a Wall's Dalek Death Ray lolly when you put it in a microwave?'

Aellini shook his head, awestruck at the Doctor's ability to combine the essential with the absurdly frivolous. 'Not really, no.'

'Thought so,' the Doctor shot back, miming a splattered explosion with his face and hands. 'Didn't notice that many ice-cream vendors on Belannia VIII.'

Aellini shook his head, gathered the medical team and began to issue instructions. 'Stay in touch. Monitor each other at all times. We'll rope up if we need to. I don't want anyone taking any chances. We've lost enough people here already today and I don't want to add to their…'

The Doctor waited, leaning into the wind and tapping his feet impatiently for a few moments, then simply turned away and began to walk.

'Doctor! Where do you think you're going?'

Without turning the Doctor called back, 'If this is what the conditions are like at night, think what the force will be like when the sun comes up.' He consulted a pocket watch. 'Sunrise is in forty minutes.' He put away the watch. 'Life's a big adventure Mr Aellini. If you talk about what you're going to do for too long you miss the chance to do it!'

Somehow, despite the wind and the lack of radio, his words carried clearly to everyone. Aellini frowned. Smoot had told him the Doctor would be trouble. Well. No one could be more trouble than the side arm holstered at his waist.

Aellini at the head of the column, the medical team began to plod after the Doctor, now bounding goat-like across the rocks and intermittently vanishing among the rain-lashed darkness.

Following his nose, the Doctor found the first crash site less than thirty minutes later. It was Conaway's ship. Wreckage was strewn over a large area. The bulk of the vessel was wedged in a gully, its impact clearly cushioned by the burned and broken remains of storm-swept trees. There were no bodies.

There was one survivor.

They found her huddled in the tool locker in the remains of the payload bay, almost delirious with shock but otherwise mercifully uninjured.

The Doctor waited for the medical team to finish, made a cursory examination himself and then crouched beside the woman. Outside, the storm boomed. Flaps of hull creaked and squealed as they were peeled away by the remorseless wind. The planet was flaying the ship alive. What might it do to any human out unprotected in it? What might it do to Conaway?

'You want to know where they are, right?' The woman tried to crawl away from the Doctor. She banged her shoulder on the metal door of the locker and fell over. She began to cry. 'It took them. The planet came and *the planet came and it took them it took them all away*!'

Pain.

Sam was beginning to think it was the only real thing in her life any more.

What amazed her most – beyond the fact that she could stand it at all – was the idea that there were so many different types of it. And that all these different types could be felt at once.

The deep ache of radiation sickness, just as on Janus Prime, the sharp stabbing pains of decompression, the freezing numbness of ice burn – her body was a carnival freak show of capering agony.

And her skin: motile, healing, decaying, healing, decaying…

And, if her body waxed and waned more dramatically than the tides, what of her mind? What corner of her consciousness was there that remained protected from the pain? None, for the human body is a wonderful machine which takes every opportunity to warn itself when things are not right.

Things were not right with Sam Jones. Oh no. Not by a long chalk.

Things might not ever be right again.

She had died. She knew that. The lack of air had caused her to suffocate. The wind-chill factor alone would have reduced her to a frozen corpse in moments, the radiation lashing the surface a slower but infinitely more horrible death.

All these deaths she had suffered many times since her conversion. Her mind shied from the terror of cancer exploding through her body only to be itself destroyed; of skin frozen to the point of peeling away only to be made whole again; molecules brought under control, a flux of life, the pain burning away death and life together until there was nothing left but the pain. And it was she and she was it, a living thing made of pain; it crept in her blood, it moved tirelessly through her muscles, her lymphatic system, her lungs and other organs. Her heart and mind were filled with it. Her nervous system sang hymns to it.

Her voice rose as her sanity began slowly to leach away, rose to join the chorus of others in an unconscious and uncontrollable prayer of pain to their god, the priest who sat humbly at their head, contemplating his own Endless State.

Sam waited to faint.

She didn't.

She waited to die.

She didn't.

She waited to go mad.

She didn't.

After several hours she realised she was bored. Bored of the pain. Bored of the fact that she was scared.

She grinned, felt her smile crack and be repaired almost as quickly.

She got up. Walked to the nearest wall, broke off a shard of ice and drove it deep into her throat.

Her scream brought a momentary silence to the prayer of the Endless.

The scream bubbled away into silence.

She did not die.

She dropped the shard.

Sat down.

Stood up.

She did not die.

Blinked eyelids blackened with frostbite, felt the bruises evolve through her flesh.

Grinned again.

She could not die.

But what *could* she do?

I don't want to spend eternity here in this hell of ice. I want to spend it in a nice place. Warm. Where the cars are red and fit like gloves, where petrol is free, where girls don't die, and all choices work out; where there are nice carpets and ice lollies are cool and TV doesn't have any adverts. And food! Foooooooood! That would be sooooooo nice.

Sam turned to the congregation, aware the blood had stopped flowing from her throat. Her voice was the screech of rusted metal as she said, 'Listen. To. Me. We. Have. To. Get. Off. This. Place. Eternity. Doesn't. Have to… hurt. I can help you… Do you see? I can get you food – even ham. Green eggs and ham for everyone. You can have them with foxes in boxes, or fishes on dishes. All we have to do is make the ship work. Then we can leave here. Do you see?'

The congregation gazed blankly at her, then, one by one, resumed their hymn of pain.

All except one.

Denadi rose to his feet, his face twisted, his body arched within his sealed starsuit.

Denadi who would not take communion and who would now die for the privilege when his air ran out.

Sam stumbled across to him.

His lips moved. Shaped her name. Silent whisper. *Sam…*

'I am Sam,' she said. 'Sam I –' She stopped. Bit her lip. Bit it even harder as it began immediately to heal.

Denadi's face inside the helmet was the face of a tortured angel. Death held no peace for him. She caught him as he fell, felt his body jerk as life left it.

Saketh's voice moved restlessly among the blue ice. 'Endless. He is Endless now. But he is wrong. His way is wrong.'

Sam laid Denadi on the ground.

Brain (ham) death –

– how long did it take (to cook) for all higher functions to end?

Sam struggled to keep it clear in her mind. The taste of ham between her teeth was a fantasy, a mustard-coated slice of heaven. Denadi was a dead weight in her arms. No. She'd laid him on the – no she had – no she was –

– taking off his helmet.

'Eat of my ham – my *flesh*.' She said. 'Drink of my blood.'

He did not hear her.

He did not move.

'I can help you. *I can help you! Father, don't die now! Oh God, don't leave me alone here!*'

But she couldn't.

It was too late.

The choice was yours all the time. She seemed to hear the words in his voice, but it might have just been the wind.

She felt a presence beside her. Saketh. Unmistakably him. She did not turn.

'Brain death takes several minutes. You can bring him back. Was it what he wanted?'

Sam did not hesitate. 'Yes! He told me just before he… as I was holding him… his last words were… he wanted to take communion with us. He wanted to convert. He told me!'

Not for one moment did Sam understand how damning the lie that would save the life of Denadi was to be.

Sunrise came to the new world in a kaleidoscopic iteration of life.

Things that might have been birds or fish flapped or swam through the air. They made a sound that was indescribable. It might have been laughter or machine noise. No one could tell. More life crawled and flapped across the surface. Again, no one could tell if this life was vegetable or animal – motile seeds seeking fertile ground or animals seeking to evade a vegetable predator. The world was a circus mirror of a real world, one in which the reflecting surface was constantly evolving, unbending, flattening with time, before assuming some new, evolutionary kink.

The rain stopped, then started again. The clouds changed colour as volcanic gases emerged to mingle with the sunlight. Yellow blotches of sulphur appeared on the ground. Some of them had legs and fled from the approaching heavy tread of the medics' starsuits.

Mud steamed and popped diligently.

The Doctor was like a child in Santa's grotto. He capered gleefully among the often near-lethal volcanic upheavals, the clogging vegetation, the shifting geology. His hands clutched a small device which he waved around himself every so often, as if to capture elements of the scenery for later observation.

Aellini questioned him on this. 'Is that some kind of tracker you've got there?'

'No, no! No, bless me, no!' The Doctor laughed out loud, his words an excited torrent, tumbling over themselves in their eagerness to escape. 'Polaroid camera! Never seen a world being born before! Wanted a few snaps for the album!' He leaned closer to Aellini's helmet and said in a confidential stage whisper, 'You never know what the parents might pay for a shot like this...'

Aellini felt anger build. 'Lives are at stake here.'

'Never doubted it!' the Doctor mumbled cheerfully. He held his breath as a cloud of sulphurous steam clogged the air for several minutes, then blew out his cheeks. His face, hair and coat were bright yellow. He shook his head and the sulphur flew off. Aellini scraped more of it from his faceplate, studying the Doctor as he did so. The man was at home here – almost as if he had been born here. He could cope with every change of air, every poisonous belch with no effort at all. Chemical combinations that even the starsuits had a hard time dealing with slipped from his clothes and skin like so much colourful confetti. Major Smoot was right to have been suspicious. Aellini was getting a very strange feeling about the Doctor. As if he were... somehow... *luring* them somewhere. If it weren't for the fact that he always seemed to know exactly where their own tracking devices indicated they should go a moment or two before the devices actually surrendered that information – no: as a matter of fact, the fact that he knew their direction before they did actually made the Doctor's actions and behaviour even more suspicious.

Aellini waited for a moment alone to check the magazine on his sidearm. Fully charged. Good. Aellini had never yet met an enemy who could deal with *that*.

The trail led to a chasm carved in a gigantic cliff face. The Doctor turned to Aellini and cheerfully asked if he had any rope.

Aellini sighed, grabbed the Doctor and activated his starsuit's jets. He hoped they would not need to go too far. The suit jets were designed for short bursts in zero-gravity conditions. Planet hopping was not only dangerous but frighteningly expensive on fuel.

The Doctor's eyes opened wide with excitement as they dropped over the lip of the chasm.

He peered around himself as they dropped.

'Interesting,' he said as he pulled his opera glasses once again from a pocket and examined the cliff face through them. 'No fossil record that I can see.'

'So? Maybe it was all destroyed by geological activity.'

'Nonsense. Every planet has a geological record. Unless…' He peered thoughtfully through the glasses.

'Unless what?' Aellini muttered in irritation.

'Unless it's not a planet, of course.'

Aellini found he didn't have anything to say to that.

Almost immediately he found that he did. But he didn't say it. He thought it though: If it's not a planet what is it? A spaceship? A hostile invasion spearhead? It could hold billions of aliens. What kind of aggressor used an entire species as its assault force?

He looked back up the chasm, was not quite comforted by the fighter escort's triple contrail poking through the rain clouds.

The cavern closed overhead as the interior of the planet – spaceship? – wrapped itself around them in intimate folds.

The cavern system was deep, a three dimensional labyrinth in which the only clue to direction was gravity, and even that a feeble one.

The Doctor's nose – and Aellini's computer information – led the medical party to a small grotto about half a kilometre deep in the crust. The rock here was spongy, almost springy. It had a sense of newness about it. Aellini wondered whether the hull of this world-ship was organic in nature, grown to meet the shifting extremes of temperature it must find on its journey through space.

The survivors – twelve in all – were in the cavern. They were comatose, their faces twitching with REM sleep.

Aellini wondered what they were dreaming about.

The Doctor carefully peered into the faceplate of each starsuit. Conaway was not among them.

Aellini began issuing instructions. 'I want Fighter Escort One to stand by at the mouth of the cavern. I want the drone carrier brought here on remote so we can load these people aboard the moment we hit the surface. Now let's snap to it. The mission's not over until we bring these people home.'

The Doctor placed a hand on the shoulder of Aellini's starsuit. 'The mission's not over until we find Surgeon Major Conaway.'

Aellini sighed angrily. 'Face it, Doctor, she's dead. It's bad, I know. But we have to get these people out. They are our priority now.'

'The Chinese on Earth have a proverb.' In the rocky gallery, the Doctor's voice sounded slightly more dangerous than an earthquake. 'Save someone's life and become responsible for it.'

'You can't save her if she's not here.'

The Doctor's expression was unreadable. 'Oh, I'm not talking about Major Conaway. I've saved more than a hundred billion people in the last few days. It's them I'm being responsible to. Major Conaway is the icing on the cake, so to speak. But I have a much bigger responsibility than to the life of one person, no matter how precious. An older me would have sacrificed the one for the other; an even older me might not have acknowledged that the one existed. I'm different now. I'm younger, more mature. Somehow I have to be responsible for both the individual and the whole. Do you see?'

'Frankly, I think you're raving mad.'

'Nero was mad. Genghis Khan was mad. Hitler was mildly paranoid. I, on the other hand, am merely very, very concerned.

About a great many things, Mr Aellini,' he added, anticipating the pilot's question. 'A very great many things indeed.'

And with that he turned and followed his nose from the gallery, in search of his friend, the other doctor.

He found her twenty minutes later, at the nexus of what seemed to be a mass of vegetable fibre, trapped in a maze of growth that held her as fast as any straitjacket.

Her eyes were open but unseeing, focused instead on some inner world of nightmarish revelation.

The Doctor reached for her automatically, his intention to pull her clear. Instead, he found himself gripped by hands curled like talons, his body and mind caught as she was herself, arching fearfully as a lifetime of memories smashed home into his mind. A lifetime whose heartbeats were measured by the lives of stars.

With it came madness.

No one wanted to help her. They all just stayed in the grotto, content to wait for Saketh's leadership. Content to endure the pain that was their personal eternity, content to allow themselves no choice in being saved. To Sam they were a girl lying comatose in a hospital A&E, waiting to die while her father let it happen.

Sam shrugged. It was their choice. She had work to do.

Lots of work.

How many were there left in the solar system who had not been touched by the breath of immortality?

Millions?

Billions?

She could help them all.

She would start with the Hoth. It at least was close. But how should she get to it? How to cross space from this moon to the atmosphere of Belannia XII?

The ship that brought her here was the answer: empty, power-drained, fuel all but exhausted in its fight against the freezing ocean in which it lay; it was an answer of sorts.

Sam worked inside it now, the freezing swim down through the icy currents forgotten as her body healed quickly, the pain fading slightly as her lungs responded to the minimal air in the circulation system, the minimal heat remaining in the environment-control systems.

Sam worked to reduce even that, diverting power steadily through shunts and busses never designed to take the load, from any peripheral system she could find, all into the main drive units.

At last the ship was ready. There was no heat or air – Sam did not need any. The pain began to creep back again, steadily building as she surveyed the wreckage of the bridge stations that was her work.

There was light, minimal, enough so that she could see to work – and she begrudged even that. But it was little enough, this one illumination. There was power enough to do what she had to do.

Footsteps clanged as she ran the power up to full. She turned as the ship quivered into life, turned to face another on the bridge.

Denadi.

'*Why?*' The priest was furious. 'You brought me back! What right did you have to do that?'

Sam smiled. '"… death is among us… but do not fear… death is our friend… death frees us from the prison of our lives… death is the doorway to our Endless State…"'

Denadi's face twisted with horror as he recognised the words of his own sermon quoted out of context.

'How wrong you were, Father. I always knew this in my heart – that religion was wrong. All you do is take away people's choices.'

'You don't understand. People make their own choices. You did.

I did. You altered my choice.'

'I saved you.' Sam thought back to a time that seemed so long ago that it was a distant memory. 'You saved me. Now I have saved you.'

'You damned me.'

'I gave you life. I gave you the Endless you so desired.'

'*You have kept me from heaven!*'

'There is no heaven any more,' Sam said mildly. 'Perhaps there never was, except in your scriptures.'

Denuded bunched his hands into bear's fists, his bulky body hunched, a combination of anger and despair. 'You do not understand. You are but a child! Your mind is young and now it is Endless. You are not ready for eternity. You do not understand the responsibilities.'

'Oh, I think I do. Why else do you think I repaired the ship?'

Denadi's face twisted in confusion. 'The refugees –'

'– have their own ship. How else did Saketh arrive here? They remain in this moon of their own choice. I offered them freedom, I offered them green ham and eggs. Did they listen to me? No. Well. That was their choice. I have other work to do.'

Denadi bit his lip. Blood flowed – briefly. 'Work?'

'Yes. Work, Father. No doubt you are familiar with the concept. I must pass on the Message. The Message of Life Eternal.'

'To whom would you pass it?' There was real fear in Denadi's voice now.

'Why, to everyone of course.'

'And if they chose not to accept?'

Sam shook her head wearily. 'Most people are powerless to make choices for themselves, Father. I have seen this. But I know the right choice to make. I can save everyone. I can show them the truth.'

Denadi seemed to crumple. 'If you believe that you are truly damned.'

Sam smiled, the newly healed skin crinkling. 'I am liberated,' she said in a whisper. 'I am the liberator. I am the light. Well... I say let there *be* light, in this dark old universe!' Incredibly she laughed. 'What do you say, Father? Shall we shine a little light? What about a little love?' She repeated the words, singing them this time, a twenty-year-old pop song lodged inescapably in her mind. ' "Shine a little love on my life – ooh – ooh – ooh!" '

She grabbed the controls and yanked hard on the stick. Nothing happened.

She blinked, thought for a moment, then told the computer to take off.

The ship quivered, lurched upward, leapt clear of the ice. Glowing holes contracted in the surface behind it, showered with fountains of slush and broken ice.

Denadi watched her at the controls and his mind recoiled in horror. Horror at what she was, horror at what she had made him, horror at the fact that she thought it was right.

Sam just kept on singing.

Somewhere, the song became a litany; she was raving, her voice a delusional hymn: a torrent of words spilled from her lips, prayers to the god of broken minds.

She was quite mad.

' "Shine a little love on my life – and let me see!" '

She was still singing the same tune an hour later when she angled the ship towards a new gravity well, opened the engines up to full throttle and drove steeply downward into the killing atmosphere of Belannia XII.

Chapter Eight

Symbiosis.

The sum function of a child and its parents.

Growth.

Life beyond death.

A kind of immortality.

The Doctor gazed at his body. Not beautiful – quirky. Attractive, yes, but to her it was so much biological machinery. Form with a very specific function. In his case the function was less than perfect.

She was puzzled. So far the pregnancy had gone without a hitch. Why the complication now? Why this late?

There was always a reason. Drug factors, disease factors, violence, sometimes just plain old-fashioned bad luck.

The patient was in pain. She ordered his spinal block increased. They were hovering dangerously near the point where anaesthesia would have to be discontinued. Full anaesthesia was out of the question for obvious reasons – she needed a conscious patient to deliver this infant. But delivery was turning out to be a big problem. She turned to a nurse and ordered the preparation of a section set. If a Caesarean was the only answer she would perform it unhesitatingly. But the time was not quite yet.

A moment or two.

She called for a blood-pressure reading.

The answer worried her.

She placed a gloved hand on his swollen belly. If his kicks were

anything to judge by the kid was going to be a centre forward.
If he made it through the next few minutes.

That addition to the thought caused her to glance at the nurse. 'Prep for Caesarean. We're going to have to do this the hard way.'

The Doctor felt the blade that opened him, felt it on a level deeper than the anaesthesia could prevent, felt it almost at the level of atoms. He was intensely in tune with his body. Knew it intimately; felt the molecular dance of skin and fat and muscle interrupted by sharp steel at body temperature.

When they took the baby from him it was as if they had taken a part of his very soul.

The Doctor worked hard to close the opening in his belly – quickly but methodically sealing, stitching, keeping his life intact.

She felt her brow mopped as she worked. Good team. Trustworthy. Reliable.

She reached a break point, stood back, allowed the surgical assistant to close. She turned then. She had a second patient now.

The infant's life signs were weak.

She cradled the new life in her hands, cupped fingers as big as its whole body.

She moved quickly towards the incubator.

He raised his head painfully from the table; his last desire as the full anaesthesia took hold was to see the baby. He fought the drugs, the scream of foreign material holding the new opening in his body together. He struggled to rise, managed to lift his head a few centimetres from the table.

The baby was alive. Cupped in the Doctor's hands, his baby was alive! He saw its arms waving, heard its voice crying for attention.

Was it a boy or girl? He couldn't tell.

'Love you,' he whispered happily as the Doctor put the squealing infant tenderly into the red giant star.

The rescue ship drove down into the heart of Belannia XII. It screeched like an animal, hunted and ripped by the storms girdling the planet. Lightning crackled. Bolts of life, smashing out of the sky with the force of colliding worlds. The atmosphere was a soup, dense, almost metallic. It dragged at the ship, clawed ropes of liquid air grasping at the vessel, fingers piercing the hull and peeling it greedily away.

Thunder boomed, emotion-twisting subsonics. The hull sang a contrapuntal rhythm of imminent doom. Sam screamed with the ship. It was a scream of joy, of exultation, of terror, of invulnerability.

Down. Pedal to the metal all the way.

It was a wild ride.

Denadi grasped the already tightened seat restraints. Liquid air under hundreds of atmospheres' pressure smashed in boiling waves against the vision ports.

The hull popped. It screeched. Sam did too.

Denadi was voiceless, speechless, almost mindless with the experience. Nothing in his life had prepared him for something so totally overwhelming. He had no idea. None. He had never ridden a roller coaster. Never driven a car. The nearest he had ever come to this wild ride was a few hours' tobogganing down a shallow hill beside his mother's house one year when he was very small.

There was simply no comparison. No words. Just inarticulate noises as the ship jagged this way and that, battered by the storm, battered even further by Sam's relentless urge to test her new belief to the limit...

He managed to turn his head against the force of motion. Sam was grinning. A predatory expression better suited to an animal. Primitive pleasure/satisfaction, no higher function at all.

Almost.

Noticing his look, Sam shouted above the infernal howl of the drive engines, 'Here's my thing: we're gonna crash, right? Smash into the Hoth. It's going to eat our flesh, drink our blood. It's going to live for ever. It's going to save us in return. Symbiosis right? Life for life.'

Denadi struggled to speak.

'Listen,' Sam went on, 'I know you want ham, right? Sorry. It'll have to wait. The future's at hand, Father. And it's you and me.'

Denadi found a second to wonder what would happen if things went wrong. Would they consciously experience being smashed flat by thousands of atmospheres' pressure? Would they live for ever, a consciousness smeared together and trapped at the bottom of a gravity well they didn't have the strength to escape from? Would they die when the planet died, consumed as its sun turned nova? Of would they live, in some altered form but with continuous memories? What of the universe? Would they see its end too?

Was *that* hell?

Denadi had no time to ponder these questions.

A living form as big as a small country emerged from the mist. The Hoth.

It billowed, glowing with colour, bright against the nacreous atmosphere.

Sam increased the engines to maximum power and drove vertically down to meet it.

Aellini moved very slowly along the passage. Very, very slowly. He listened, the suit mikes turned up to full gain.

The conversation he could hear was interesting. Very, very interesting.

There were two voices. Both he recognised. The Doctor and Surgeon Major Conaway. They sounded drunk or drugged. Or happy.

Very, very happy.

Under the circumstances this was very, very suspicious.

He unbuttoned the safety flap on his side-arm holster, turned on the suit's voice recorder and moved closer.

Conaway worked on automatic. She rose, examined herself, found no broken bones, only the memories of a lifetime. She was sweating, her body racked with fatigue. It was as if she'd *lived* that entire alien lifetime in a few moments.

She looked around. The Doctor lay beside her on the ground. She moved to him, her muscles protesting wildly at even this simple action. She touched his skin. It was icy cold. 'Doctor, come on, wake up!' He stirred, his eyes wandering unfocused, in several different directions. 'Are you all right? Look at me! How many fingers am I holding up?'

The Doctor blinked rapidly. He looked at her fingers. '"The Ride of the Valkyries" was a commercial gimmick designed solely to garner publicity for Wagner's *Ring* cycle during performances considerably shorter than its own epic length,' he pronounced with utter authority and absolutely no relevance whatsoever.

Conaway looked at her fingers once just to make sure he wasn't seeing something she wasn't, and then shook her head. She placed her fingers at his neck, searching for a carotid pulse. She found three.

The Doctor threw back his head at her touch. 'My baby! Where's my –'

The sound of her slap echoing in the cavern shocked Conaway as much as it must have shocked the Doctor.

He said mournfully, 'Ah. D'you know, there's nothing quite like the abrupt and violent juxtaposition of the open palm with the *facies bucca* to facilitate a state of greater mental awareness.'

Conaway smiled. 'I can give you another slap round the face if you think it's necessary.'

The Doctor bounced upright, swaying and wearing the same distant, slightly bemused expression as a jack-in-the-box might. 'Oh no, thank you Surgeon Major, that won't be necessary. One of your slaps is more than ample.'

'Good.' Conaway got to her feet, and allowed more of her recent memories to surface. 'Because we have a problem, don't we? A problem even a good slap won't fix.'

The Doctor nodded. 'I'm afraid so. Save the alien embryo gestating within the sun and it destroys the sun, the solar system and everything in it when it's born. Save the system – and the embryo is never born. The future of an entire species weighed against all other life in this solar system.'

'Talk about a rock and a hard place.'

'Hardly original. But apt.'

Conaway thought for a moment. 'We could attempt to communicate again. Maybe we could find out if the aliens themselves could help us.'

The Doctor frowned. He waved his arms around at the massive web of organic matter in which they were both still tangled.

'These nerve clusters are as big as transatlantic telephone cables. I suspect that to an alien the size of a planet we probably don't even exist.'

Conaway nudged a nearby rope of flesh distractedly. 'But surely – there was a communication. We experienced part of its life. Mating. A birth.'

'The *first* birth.'

Conaway continued, 'Surely there would be some exchange, some awareness. Of us, I mean.'

The Doctor considered. 'If an ant you were standing beside tried to tell you not to step sideways so you wouldn't step on it by accident do you think you'd notice its attempts? And, if you did, do you think you'd understand them?'

Conaway let her hands fall idly back to her sides. 'I see your point. But if I did notice I could infer meaning. I'm not stupid.'

'Yes, but what about the aliens? Just because you're as big as a planet doesn't necessarily mean you're concurrently intelligent.'

'True enough.'

The Doctor continued, 'Merely on the physical scale I was talking about, it would be akin to your noticing that one of the molecules in your body wanted to have a friendly chat.'

Conaway found herself nodding. 'It wouldn't be as if we'd have anything in common, right?'

'Precisely.'

Conaway tried to dispel the introspective mood her recent experience and current conversation were generating. 'So your point is?'

The Doctor wriggled his eyebrows at one of the nerve clusters. It ignored him completely. 'Hm. Not Delphon then. Ah well. I suppose my point is that we'd better explain all this to Major Smoot and get him to cease hostilities and attempt to open lines of communication. Before something unfortunate happens.'

He turned to make his way carefully out of the cavern, then stopped. Conaway followed his gaze. Aellini was there. He was covering them with a gun. 'Something unfortunate has already happened,' he said quietly. 'I've recorded and uplinked your conversation to Major Smoot. He's not very happy about your collaboration with an enemy whose very life cycle depends on the destruction of this solar system. I'm afraid he's rerouted your gravity stabiliser satellites to high orbit, where if required they can be used to *disrupt* local gravity. They will make an excellent weapon. He believes – and I must say I agree with him – that any negotiations are better undertaken from a position of strength. He asked me to mention this only so you could pass it on to…' He smiled bleakly. 'To those who need to know.'

Sam dived for three kilometres into the Hoth before the increasing density of body mass finally caused the rescue ship to disintegrate.

By this time Denadi was experiencing something akin to religious euphoria brought about by the combination of sheer terror and unrelenting pain.

Angels. I can see angels, he thought. We are angels. We are demons too. Self-made in our own images. Life imitates art. *Oh. Mother. I want to play in the snow.*

He felt a smile crease the distorted remains of his face.

I wonder if Sam can see green ham.

Sam had stopped singing by now. Denadi was glad. He liked the tune immensely but he wasn't sure he could listen to it for the rest of his life. A life that would last roughly for ever.

Part of the reason Sam had stopped singing was that the atmospheric pressure within the Hoth was high enough to crush most metals.

It was at this point Denadi found himself wondering how they could still be alive. He had no answer.

He also realised that he could not hear or see anything. It wasn't, he realised suddenly, that there was no light or sound to bring images to his mind – it was that his body no longer contained any functioning sense organs with which to receive these signals. With this came the odd realisation that he was no longer in pain. At least, if he was, he was no longer able to differentiate the pain from any other sensory input his mind was still capable of receiving. If in fact it was receiving anything and not simply spontaneously generating its own sensory ghosts through lack of any other stimulation.

He wondered how long they had been inside the Hoth.

He wondered if they would ever get out.

He wondered what his mother would have to say about this.

He wondered how he could be wondering anything at all.

He wondered silently if he would be forgiven for falling so far from the Endless Way.

He wondered how they were going to get out of the Hoth, how they were going to get out of the atmosphere, how long they had been here.

He realised the concept of *time* was meaningless.

He had all the time in the world. All the time there ever was

this such a bad thing mother if you could only see what I am now

if you could only understand what I have
what

I

want

to

play

in

the

Hoth

moved

slowly

upwards

through

the
ocean of
life towards the
surface where it burst
free from   the restraints of
gravity   and moved away
and   folded space

                and folded

           time

and

Belannia VIII swam beneath her, a planet of light, a dazzling nimbus of radiant energy whose population had doubled in the last seven days, whose ecology and resources and systems of government were now stretched to bursting point, maintained by the thinnest of margins by a single orbiting device designed to protect the planet and keep its population and more than fifty billion refugees as safe as possible from a sun whose life was also in question.

That was what *Sam* saw.

Others saw Heaven.

For the life inside her this planet and every living thing on it was nothing more or less than *God itself*.

'Let me state the situation simply for the benefit of the hard of thinking, Major.'

The Doctor paced. He pursed his lips. He fairly shook. He was indignant, furious, despairing. How was it that humanity always managed to confound him like this? Did they think the universe was nothing more than a big sandpit for them to play in? To knock each other's little sand castles over in and trample on each other's creations?

'The planet we are in orbit around is in fact an alien life form. It's a *facilitator*, one-third of a mating triad, the other two being the so-called "planets" located at the major Trojan points along this same orbit. Now listen to me very carefully, Major. Ten million years ago these three mated and produced an offspring. The infant was deposited in the sun in order to complete its life cycle, which, under normal circumstances, would have taken something like another half a dozen million years to complete. Then your sun goes nova and the infant is born from the energy outrush. That's the theory anyway. You *changed* that when you began dumping waste into the sun. Five *centuries*, Major. That's all it took to alter the incubation cycle of a life form whose normal life span runs close on the order of that of galaxies. Can you imagine that, Major? Your insignificant little species – the bat of an eyelid in cosmic terms – creating such changes?'

Smoot said nothing. He just listened. He looked at Conaway, though. She said nothing.

The Doctor continued, 'According to Captain Aellini you have removed from orbit around Belannia VIII satellites vital to the survival of every refugee in this solar system in order to threaten the life of yet another life form. Destroy these planets – kill this life – and all hope for the infant is gone.' The Doctor's voice lowered in pitch, took on the qualities of darkest night. 'Incubation of the embryo changed the life cycle of your sun once before, a long time ago. Stillbirth, Major, will undoubtedly result in your sun turning supernova. That means extinction for you and every other living thing in this system. Now do you understand me? Do you understand what you are trying to do?'

Smoot looked again at Conaway. 'Yes, Doctor.' His face may have been unreadable but his voice made his meaning very clear. 'I know only too well.'

The Doctor noticed Conaway turn from Smoot's glance. He filed the movement for later consideration.

'Good. Because we have another problem. The aliens don't even know we're here. To them we're irrelevant – mayfly sparks on a summer evening, a brief flicker and gone. We're insignificant, Major. All they care about is their infant. But delivering their child means nova anyway – and death for this entire solar system.'

'Then, Doctor, the situation is very clear.' Smoot's expression left no doubt as to his meaning. 'If the only way to save my people is at the expense of these aliens, then regrettably – but also clearly – it is my duty to destroy them and their infant by any means necessary. However –' He hesitated. The Doctor began to speak, but Smoot ruthlessly cut him off. 'In fairness, the responsibility is mine to bear alone. You may both leave if you wish.'

Chapter Nine

Conflict was inevitable. Violence was inescapable.

When the word of what the Doctor had said spread beyond the confines of Smoot's flagship the fleet was divided. When four of the higher-ranking officers decided the Doctor was talking sense and approached the major with the intention of trying to convince him that an alternative to destruction might be possible they were imprisoned without an audience. The captains of their respective ships persuaded others to back them and the fleet was divided. Add to that the remains of the pacifist ships which Smoot had already tried to destroy and respectable number of ships were now in opposition to the bulk of the fleet. Although they were outnumbered almost three to one, the renegade fleet rallied around the corvette on which the Doctor and Conaway had been transferred from the personnel transport that had carried them from the major's flagship.

Now the Doctor found himself caught in the middle as a large military force laid plans to destroy one of the most unusual life forms he had ever encountered, and a slightly smaller, though no less dedicated, number of men and women laid their own plans to oppose their former commander – with their lives if necessary, it appeared.

The truth of the situation was an ironic cruelty he had no trouble at all understanding: he was as much a prisoner of the situation he thought he could solve as he had been aboard Smoot's flagship – and equally powerless.

Now he gazed out of the observation ports of the corvette gallery and shook his head sadly.

'They were right. Best intentions never excuse the mess you leave behind.'

Beside him, Conaway watched the mass of grey, block-shaped vessels take up a defensive formation. 'Feeling sorry for yourself?'

The Doctor bit his lip. 'I once left a world because I disagreed with the philosophy of its Masters.'

'And now?'

'I still disagree with it. But… I have to agree, sometimes they're right. As soon as you interfere… things invariably get worse.'

'So you're just going to stand here and let it happen.'

The Doctor's voice snapped angrily. 'I caused it, Surgeon Major. I built the gravity generators. I put the sword in the barbarian's hands.'

Conaway sighed. 'And you told him where the enemy was sleeping.'

'Caught on the horns of my own dilemma. Even if I could warn the enemy it wouldn't mean anything. What do planets know of the violence of people?'

Conaway said quietly, 'Tell that to the ecologists.'

The Doctor laced his fingers, unlaced them, pressed his hands against the window glass. One hand blotted out the entire planet. A fingertip obscured twelve ships. 'It's a matter of distance.' His voice was slow, dreamy and dark. 'I can't keep the distance. I never have been able to. I sometimes wonder whether the universe has special designs on me. A catalyst. A shaper of destiny.'

Conaway moved closer. 'Don't be a sucker for your own depression,' she said gently. 'You made a mistake. OK, maybe you've made lots of mistakes. The thing is to figure out what can you do about it now.'

The Doctor made no attempt to move away. 'Spoken like a true lifesaver.'

'It's my job.'

'Then we appear to be opposite sides of life's two-headed Martian penny.'

Conaway laughed aloud. 'I figured you out, you know that? Man of mystery? Man of destiny? Nope. Man of bloody nonsense. Get off your arse and do something. Do it now.' Her face bloomed in the sudden glow of missile fire. A moment later the first ship exploded. 'I've run out of bandages.'

Belannia XIII was not simply in the mess Sam had left it. It was a nightmare of demonic proportions. It was an eight-thousand-mile diameter Malthusian Event waiting to happen. Extinction was the word on everyone's lips. The refugees had overflowed from the spaceports. Temporary camps had been set up in more rural areas. These had filled in a matter of days. Human life was a virus multiplying across the planet's surface in an unstoppable wave. More and more and more refugees touched down, ignoring spaceguard warnings that there was no room and no way to provide food, straining the ecology even further. Fifty billion new arrivals landed on Belannia XIII in five days.

Then Major General Smoot took the gravity generators from three inhabited worlds and the number tripled overnight.

The chaos was indescribable. Fighting, already widespread, became virtually universal. Cities were looted, towns sacked. Human nature. The nature of the beast. It was unstoppable. Individual identity no longer existed. Just massive group entities motivated by fear, by hunger and terror.

Into this seething hell of people came a living being the size of a small country. It entered the atmosphere causing storms to rage throughout one entire hemisphere. When the Hoth landed in the largest ocean, the wave that resulted wrecked hundreds of miles of beach on several continents and killed thousands – a sacrifice necessary to ensure the Endless State of more than a hundred billion.

Sam had arrived.

Salvation had arrived.

'Eat of my flesh, drink of my blood,' she told the terrified survivors as the planet itself shook beneath a strain it could never take. 'I can save you.'

Immortality spread like a disease.

The time of epiphany was very, very near.

The new worlds moved closer in towards the sun. Major Smoot's military machine moved with them, jockeying for the best position in which to orbit the commandeered gravity stabilisers.

Opposing them, the smaller fleet slowly lost ground, ships and lives.

From inside the corvette, the Doctor and Conaway watched helplessly.

'You have to help. There has to be something we can do.'

To say Conaway was angry was an understatement of epic proportions and the Doctor knew it. 'There are many things we can do. But which is best? That's the question.'

'Stop prevaricating!'

'Actually, I'm more nearly philosophising. Choice, you see. It's all about choice. Do I have the right to make a choice that will affect others whose choice I will remove?'

Conaway flinched as a nearby ship split open, emptying its human contents into space like so much trash. 'My first mission on medical rescue was to a plague zone. We had a choice. Either everyone died or… we allowed the infection to run its course in a chosen few so that a cure could be found in time to save others.'

'What was your choice?'

'Do you need to ask?'

'The deaths of a few bought the lives of many. No, Surgeon Major. I don't need to ask.'

The Doctor still had his hands pressed flat against the window glass. Conaway enclosed one of the hands in her own. 'The only choice you have is to save lives. Save as many lives as you can. If it's all you can do then at least do that.'

The Doctor sighed. 'I can't do that. All life is important. All life. Who am I to judge the relative worth of living beings? How can I judge, even if I were able to do so? Can't you see? They were right. I can't interfere. I mustn't!'

Conaway gripped the Doctor's hand even more tightly. 'How can you not? This situation is your fault. You say you put the sword in the barbarian's hand. Well – surely the least you could do is take away the sword.'

The Doctor seemed almost paralysed. He shook. It was as if every muscle in his body was getting conflicting instructions about where to move. He shivered. His voice was a hoarse whisper. 'I... can't... work... it... out!'

The door to the galley opened as the Doctor fell silent. Conaway turned. She saw a tall man, horribly scarred, whose skin seemed to move of its own accord in subtle fashion. His voice, when he spoke, was the sound of all her fears and all her hopes.

'I am told the Doctor is here. I'm looking for him. It's about Sam.'

The Doctor turned. His face was a portrait of despair. 'Oh no. Is she... ?'

'No. She is alive.'

The Doctor released a breath he did not even realise he was holding. 'But she's in trouble, though?'

'She is Endless.'

'That sounds like trouble enough.'

Conaway looked from one man to the other. 'Doctor, you don't have time for this! You're supposed to be helping here!'

The Doctor snapped, 'I *can't* help here!' He looked back at the newcomer. 'Mr…?'

'Father. Eldred Saketh.'

'Father Saketh. Tell me everything you can about Sam.'

The story unfolded slowly, deliberately, a parable related to the accompaniment of bright flashes of death outside the corvette vision ports. Every so often the ship itself would shake, battered by a debris flung clear from a nearby detonation.

Saketh's voice meshed with the rumble of engines, the atonal boom and clash of machinery, the thud and screech of straining hull.

The Doctor found himself drawn into the story. He lived the pain, the hopes and fear, the glorious madness that was his new friend. *Oh, Sam. All you ever wanted to be was a grown-up.*

Eventually there were no more words. Saketh fell silent.

The Doctor considered. 'You are immortal.'

It wasn't a question. Saketh felt no need to answer. Instead he offered a deal. 'You cannot get to your gravity stabilisers because you will be killed if you do. I cannot be killed. Tell me how to reprogram them and I will place them back in orbit around the planets where they belong. While I am doing this you can find Sam. You can help her. She needs you, Doctor. Needs you very badly.'

Conaway stared wildly from one man to the other. 'You're not thinking of doing as he says?'

'"The only choice you have is to save lives. Save as many lives as you can. If it's all you can do then at least do that."' The Doctor's voice was cold – almost as cold as Conaway's face as she listened to her own words quoted back to her. 'What other *choice* do I have?'

It was her time. Sam's time. The time of forever.

War was over. Violence at an end.

With eternity came peace.

By the time the Doctor arrived almost three-quarters of the population could not die.

He found her on a long stretch of beach, a tiny island in an ocean of humanity. Acolytes, worshippers – the laity of her new faith. She sat on a wooden chair beneath a cane shelter and surveyed everything that was hers, everything she had built. On a small table in front of her was a platter, its contents covered by a silver dome.

The people were all sitting. They were absolutely silent. Though there were many thousands of them, the Doctor had to strain to catch even the faintest breath, the slightest movement above the lapping of waves and the distant, indignant squeal of a lone gull. He worked his way slowly through the outskirts of the crowd. Heads turned towards him. They knew he was an outsider. Sensed it somehow. No one moved to stop him as he approached the shelter. But he felt thousands of pairs of eyes turn upon him with more than mere interest.

He picked a way through the crowd, stepping over children and seated adults, hopping between tiny patches of clear ground as if they were stepping stones in a river turned to a sheet of ice by winter. In this manner he proceeded and, after a time, he reached the cane shelter. He stood in the relatively narrow band of clear ground before her and waited. She did not speak, though her eyes had followed his every movement as he had approached.

'Sam,' he said after a silence that was merely uncomfortable had stretched to unbearable length. 'Sam Sam Sam Sam Sam. It's me.'

She looked at him for a long moment before recognition dawned. 'Doctor.' She smiled. 'I'm so pleased to see you.'

'And I you, Sam. More than you can know.'

Another long pause. Sam surveyed the crowd. They were utterly silent, tiny breaths from the newly converted gradually becoming more sporadic.

The Doctor felt the collective gaze of the laity strike him between the shoulder blades and the weight was all but overwhelming.

His skin crawled.

He waited.

An hour passed.

Sam returned her gaze to him.

He waited.

She beckoned him forward.

He moved slowly towards the cane shelter.

'Sit.'

He sank cross-legged into the lotus position.

'I'd offer you tea. I don't have any.'

'What's under the dish?'

'You'd laugh.'

The Doctor ventured a smile. 'Actually I'm not that thirsty.'

'Why are you here?' There was an odd, almost disjointed quality to Sam's words.

'Don't you know?'

'To stop me? You're too late.'

'Stop you? Now… why… would I want to do that, Sam?'

'No reason, considering what I've done.'

'What have you done?'

'I've brought a world to its senses.'

'Some might say you've brought a world to its knees.'

'A matter of semantics. It amounts to the same thing.'

'Does it?'

Sam shrugged. 'My opinion doesn't actually matter very much either. When you are part of the truth, understanding is not required.'

'Now that I *don't* understand.'

'You're lying. Trying to draw me out. Find out if I'm still here. If I'm still me. The *me* you remember.'

'All right. Hands up to that one.'

'It's fine. It doesn't matter. You can't do anything to me. I walk in eternity now.'

The Doctor shuddered.

Sam said, 'I notice you haven't pressed the point.'

'Well, you did rather answer it.'

'You think I'm insane.'

'Or possessed.'

'I'm not. I'm Sam. Sam I am.' She lifted the silver dish. 'Do you like green eggs and ham?'

The Doctor bit his lip.

'You see?' Sam replaced the dish, covering the slowly reanimating corpse of a seagull. 'I said you'd laugh.'

The Doctor suddenly bounced to his feet. 'Sam!' he yelled harshly. 'You don't like ham. Never have! You hate it because your mother packed ham sandwiches for school lunches every day until you were eight years old! You don't like eggs either, green or yellow or sky-blue-pink! You don't like anything anyone else makes you do! So why are you doing this? Why have you *done* this? I want to understand. I want to help you.'

Sam made no overt reaction to the Doctor's change in manner. Neither did anyone else. 'You cannot help me.'

'That depends on what you mean by help.' The Doctor's voice was a cold whisper. 'At least… according to Saketh it does.'

Sam's eyes narrowed. The Doctor noticed this and it made him feel uncomfortable. Something about Sam was different. He snapped his fingers mentally. She *was* different. Her skin, the placement of her features – all were perfect. The textbook perfection of art, a poetic composition of humanity. She was still herself – but she was perfect now. The narrowing of eyes denoting interest had been enough to throw off the symmetry, to make him aware of the finest of physical changes being subtly wrought on her body.

Oh, Sam.

'What do you mean?'

The Doctor shrugged. He had her interest now. What to do with it – that was the question. 'Saketh asked me to come here.'

At the sound of the name there was a rush as of wind. A collective sigh from the thousands sitting oddly still nearby. The Doctor licked his lips. 'Sam… do you remember being born?'

Sam frowned. Perfection marred a further notch.

The Doctor pressed on, 'Do you remember *why* you were born?'

Sam blinked. 'I… there is no reason why we are born. We just are. That's life. We're born. We live. We…' She stopped.

The Doctor said, 'Go on.'

'We… we…'

The Doctor shook his head. 'Tell me about growing up. Becoming a woman. What was it you most wanted? Do you remember we talked about it? A long time ago. In the TARDIS. On the beach. Do you remember?'

'I… children?'

'Are you asking me or telling me?'

'I wanted children. I wanted a child. I wanted to feel it growing inside me. I wanted to feel how I would be different. I... um... I wanted to feel the pain because it would mean I was able to make life. To give life.' Her frown suddenly cleared. Perfect Sam was back again. 'I have done this. I have given life. Saketh showed me how. Eat of my flesh and drink of my blood.'

'Yes. Quite. Do that and you have a little bit of me inside you. Enough to spread the infection.'

'*Eternity is not a disease!*'

'Tell that to the Time Lords, Sam. Call it a... function then. A by-product.'

'Of what?'

He had her. 'Of life. Life that seeks to discover what else there is. Life that lives and grows and searches for answers. That searches for God.'

Sam nodded. Still with him. Good.

'Life that swarms in its microscopic billions throughout other, more complex, life systems. Living entities themselves becoming hosts, providing energy and in return... they are kept alive. To serve as incubators. For the billions to come.'

'I don't... understand.'

'"Understanding is not required." Wasn't that what you said?'

'I...'

The Doctor moved closer, took Sam's chin in his hands. 'And there's another thing. You keep using this pretension to the first person that really isn't necessary any more. Not for any of you. Is it?'

Suddenly the Doctor's fingers dug into Sam's face. She gasped with pain but did not pull away. The Doctor stepped back. Watched as the wounds his fingers had left in her flesh healed; the skin re-forming, the bruises fading from black to healthy perfection in a matter of seconds.

'How much of Sam is left in there?'

Sam stood slowly. She seemed to be a little taller than he remembered. 'I am all Sam. Sam I am. Sam made perfect in the light of my own divinity.'

The Doctor sighed. 'I want to tell you a story.'

He waited. Nothing. He said, 'Once upon a time there was an old star. Old, red, dying. Its planets dying too. Any intelligent species born within this star's solar system had long since left. There was a storm coming, you see. A storm called *nova*. The only life remaining in this system was the shabby remnants of a once technologically proud civilisation eking out a pitiful existence on the bleak tundra that were the inner worlds. That and a handful of creatures so old, all they had left to experience was death.

'And that's how it was... until *they* arrived. No one knows who they were. No one knows why they picked this solar system in which to incubate their infant. *They* were as big as worlds. Entities whose age was almost immeasurable. Entities to whom time itself was a meaningless concept. Perhaps they weren't even from this universe at all. It doesn't matter. What mattered was that they changed things around here. They put their newly conceived infant into the old red star and gave it new life to nurse the infant.

'The result: a new, yellow sun. An impossible sun. A lease of new life running to millions of years.

'There were changes, obviously. New sun, more energy, more stable ecosystems. Evolution started all over again. This time it had two starting points: the decaying tool users... and on an inner world, a world on which radiation and heat from the newly reborn sun had wreaked unimaginable changes... the *tool* of the user.'

The Doctor waited. Sam was utterly still – perfection personified. She was like a Dresden china doll.

He said, 'It's you, Sam. Microtechnology. Molecule-sized machines. Designed to build, to repair, to renew, to alter things on a molecular level, to remove disease, to repair chromosomes... unimaginable power... trapped in the gravity well of a world close to the sun... close to dysfunction... close to death... and then... the sun *changes*. Suddenly there's heat, light, radiation, power. Billions of generations pass. Evolution takes hold here as elsewhere. Life forms itself from the primeval broth. This life has self-awareness. It processes energy. It builds copies of itself. By any definition of the word it is... *alive*. But it is trapped. Trapped in the gravity well of this dying world. Trapped as the sun swells and grows even hotter, trapped on the world that gave it birth... and which now must surely bring death.

'And then you arrive. Humans. Saketh.

'You bring the possibility of life. Of further evolution to a higher plane.

'It has found God.

'You are it, Sam.

'It saved all of you to be its God.'

He waited. Again Sam said nothing, though now there was a kind of distant look in her eyes, as though memories were surfacing there. Thoughts and images no longer her own.

The Doctor said, 'Interesting, isn't it? But this is the really important bit. Like all intelligence, this microtechnology – this microlife – has struggled to attain perfection. But evolution comes at a price. Energy is required. Huge amounts of energy. far more than could ever be produced by mere human bodies... even by planetary outputs. This new life needs more. You know what it needs, don't you, Sam? You know what frightful fiend doth this way tread. *Don't you, Sam?*'

Sam shivered. 'The sun...'

'That's right. The *sun*. All the energy you could ever want is right there, if it's released in the right way. Do that and the human hosts will no longer be required. The evolutionary destiny of the life you carry within you will have been achieved. But the cost… Oh, Sam, the terrible cost…' He waited. She seemed to be trying to speak. He uttered the words for her. 'You have done what every intelligent creature has ever done. Created a god, and allowed that god to be destroyed in your name. The cost of your evolutionary destiny is *supernova*. The death of every living thing in this system.'

Sam touched her cheek, the spot where the wound inflicted by the Doctor was no longer in evidence.

'Even now, Saketh is reprogramming the gravity stabilisers I designed. But not to protect the worlds for which they were made. Oh no. He learned from Major Smoot. It took me some time to realise his intentions. By then it was too late. I can't stop him, Sam. Nobody can. He wants to use my force for life as a weapon. A weapon to destabilise the sun. You thought he was a proponent of a Life Cult, didn't you, Sam? You were wrong. All the time you were so, so wrong. But I was wrong too. I let him use you as a weapon against me. Just goes to show you can never ignore your roots. Saketh was born in a death cult and now he'll die in one: he's holding the biggest suicidal sit-in ever. The guest list numbers two hundred billion and attendance is compulsory!'

He waited.

Nobody said anything.

Distant waves slapped against the beach.

Gulls screeched insanely as, immortal, they dived for fish they no longer needed and could not kill anyway.

Sam touched the silver dish on the table in front of her. The reflection of her finger wrapped around the metallic curve and fell out of sight. She looked up. Perfect eyes. Windows to a perfect soul?

'Do you have gods, Doctor?'

'Doesn't everyone?'

'What would you do if you ever found them? Would you question them? Doubt them? Allow them to be fallible? Would the frail vessel that is your ego allow you to interact with them at all?'

The Doctor frowned. 'I'm not sure I understand your point.'

'Would you distrust them, like you distrusted your parents, your family, your world? Would you leave them? Confront them? Force them to conform to your newly developed philosophical sophistication?' Sam waited. The Doctor said nothing. Sam continued, 'After all, people grow. Why shouldn't their gods grow with them? Should everything be destroyed in childbirth? That is not the way of the universe. If you weren't the orphan you claim you would know this.'

The Doctor said importantly, 'What I said was a *metaphor*.'

Sam said quietly, 'What I said was a metaphor too.'

The Doctor opened his mouth to make an indignant reply – then closed it again. He stared at Sam, then a thoughtful expression haunted his face. 'All right.' The Doctor's voice was low, a humble acknowledgement. 'I made an assumption about Saketh. Maybe I even made a mistake. But, if he's not planning for doomsday, what is he planning for?'

The Doctor found his own reflection in the silver dish – distorted, wrapped around and partially merged with the thin crescent of Sam's reflection.

'All right,' he said. 'What if I do nothing? What if I don't "poke my nose into other people's business"? What then?'

Sam sat motionless, unbreathing, her chest still, her skin perfect. 'Possibilities,' she said softly, drawing breath only to utter the word.

'Meaning?'

'Perhaps we'll die.'

'Or?'

'Perhaps we'll live and our gods will die.'

'Or?'

Sam waited. 'We could *become* our gods. Merge. Evolve. Give birth to a new life form. One the universe has never seen before.' She waited. 'It's just a matter of how well we understand what we are doing.'

'And what are you doing?'

Sam bit one perfect lip. The pearl of blood was perfect, and stained perfect teeth. 'What any parent would do for its child. Ensuring our future.'

The Doctor said, so softly that his voice might have been obscured by a single breath if any near had drawn one, 'And what if I can't trust you?'

Sam smiled. 'But you can.'

'But how do I know that?'

'That statement is the statement of a child. You are no longer a child. You see the possibilities. If you didn't there would be no question to ask.'

'True enough, I suppose.' The Doctor licked his lips. 'What if you make a mistake?'

'Gods do not make mistakes.'

The Doctor narrowed his eyes. 'Sam thought she was in telepathic contact with the Hoth. That was a mistake. The Hoth only remember backwards.'

Sam opened her mouth, closed it, said nothing.

Waves lapped.

The gull screeched.

Inside the silver cover, the flutter of wings grew.

The Doctor lifted the cover. The seagull burst upward. The Doctor tilted his face up to follow its movements. When he looked at Sam, she was still watching it rise into the pale, hot sky. 'Tell me your plan.'

Sam said without any preamble, 'We let the aliens bring their foetus to term and then use your devices to stabilise the sun when it goes nova. We use the energy to evolve, and leave the sun as it was when we were born – a red giant. Old, dying, true; but still capable of supporting our gods for the rest of their lives.'

'And what about Samantha Jones? The body you are in?'

'We are in many billions of bodies.'

'*I only care about one!*'

'That is a lie.'

'Is it?'

'Yes.'

'All right… yes. It's a lie. But I do care about her. Very much. She's my… she's very young.'

Sam said nothing.

'She's my *friend.*'

'She's our *god.*'

'What if I told you she was insane?'

'The price paid by a god to become mortal is high. But then that's hardly something you're unused to. Is it?'

The Doctor opened his mouth. Then closed it. Then opened it again. 'What if –'

Sam put a perfect finger to his lips. 'There are no alternatives.'

'But –'

Again Sam silenced him. 'Growth. Adulthood. It's all a matter of perception. Understanding. You and I were the same for a while. You have a little catching up to do, that's all.' She paused, then added, very quietly, 'There is only one Truth and that Truth is

239

Endless… and that Truth… is *life*. Sanity, like immortality, is just the price we have to pay.'

Chapter Ten

Riding the gravity compensator down towards the solar photosphere, Saketh gazed at the hugely swollen Bel with eyes alternately blinded and all-seeing.

He knew he had only moments to live. He had many regrets. And fears. He was Endless. He wanted to remain that way. He knew he could not. As a man he could want and fear and need. As a god, he must surrender everything he was for those who worshipped within him.

He spared one glance for the glowing dots of light that were two space-navy fleets moving rapidly away from him, the madly fluctuating Bel, the new planets even now moving to join as a precursor to the birth of their infant.

Saketh gazed into the molten light of the sun, his face shredding and re-forming, his body frozen and molten, all shape and meaning lost, except to those who prayed within.

What would happen to him at the moment of birth?

Would he at last assume an Endless State?

The proper Endless State?

Did it really matter?

Did anything matter beyond this moment?

Saketh peeled his hands from the frozen metal of the gravity stabiliser. He wanted to see them one last time. One last time before –

– the sun swelled suddenly.

Then just as suddenly contracted, sheets of flame darkening to black incandescence, invisible, ghost radiance, a final birthing scream.

His time had run out.

Amused at the ironic contradiction, Saketh laughed as he slammed his frozen, healing hands down across the control panel. He stared up at the sun, wanted to scream, knew the lack of air would prevent it.

Then the shock wave ripped across him and through him and there were no more desires, or wants, or needs or confusion.

Just his Endless State.

A state even Denadi would have accepted.

Denadi lay upon the beach of Belannia VIII and watched the sky rain sheets of fire. Beside him, ten or fifteen thousand others; beyond them, a world. More than a hundred million. All watching the sky. All waiting for their own sacrifice.

Were they all wondering, as he was, whether they would ever know anything again? Maybe today was the day they would all attain their Endless States, whether they wanted to or not.

Was that a good thing?

Who could say what good and evil were any more?

Did it matter anyway?

Did anything matter beyond this moment?

Denadi cupped his hands around a seagull. He wanted to see it heal. He wanted to see the miracle of life one last time. One last time before –

– the sun swelled suddenly.

Then just as suddenly contracted, sheets of flame darkening to black incandescence, invisible, ghost radiance, a final birthing scream.

His time had run out.

Amused at the ironic contradiction, Denadi cried as he let the seagull loose. He stared up at the sun, wanted to scream, realised he already was.

Then the shock wave ripped across him and there were no more desires, or wants, or needs or confusion.

Only life.

Normal, ephemeral life.

A life Saketh could never accept.

She watched the fireworks from the cruiser nervesphere. The shockwave smashed against the fleet. Ships collided. She heard screams. Or imagined them. Or screamed herself.

Ships burst, emptying their human cargo into the void.

Beside her Smoot braced himself against the captain's podium and remained motionless, silent. Fool. Robot. How could he remain unmoved by this moment? She knew why their marriage had never worked out. This was just further proof. He was an unfeeling, incapable, militaristic idiot without a gram of human sensitivity in his entire body. She looked at him angrily, wanting to scream at him, wanting to shout, to blast some feeling into him, to let him *see*, just for a moment, what life – any life, however short or long – was really all about. What the stakes were. What the rewards were. If you just took a chance.

He was *crying*.

Crushed, she closed her mouth.

She just watched him.

It was the birth of something new. Something she had thought she had seen before but in truth had only been lying to herself about.

She reached out and took his hand. 'Either I'm just about to make the second biggest mistake in my life,' she shrieked above the racket made by the dying ship. 'Or –'

And that was as far as she got before the sun exploded, and the largest force short of a full-blown nova ever witnessed reduced the balance of the fleet and every living thing within it to its component molecules.

Eternity was banished in a heartbeat.

From the open door of the TARDIS – freshly recovered from an infant ring system now orbiting Belannia VI – Sam watched the red star swell to blinding incandescence.

Fire gave birth to new life.

The light bathed the thousands around her, the billions more she could not see, the billions every one of them could no longer contain within their bodies.

Sam wanted to watch what happened but it all took place on a level beyond the perception of human eyes. The second most significant thing she would ever experience and she could not sense it in any way. Sam tried to decide how she felt about that. Then she decided that, far from bringing the answers, growing up simply showed you there were more questions than you could ever have imagined as a child. She wondered if she would ever find answers to even some of them. She wondered if and when she would ever get to drive that red car.

She didn't know.

After a while she realised that not knowing was part of growing up too.

She turned to go into the TARDIS – then paused. The TARDIS. She'd only really thought about it as a method of conveyance… like a car, say. Beyond this she'd never considered the implications of this peculiar blue box with a universe inside. Indestructible. That's what the Doctor had called it when she had asked how it survived the destruction of a moon. Indestructible. Eternal. Like she was herself? She puzzled over the potential similarities for a moment – a moment that, perversely, seemed to last forever. Her mind filled with questions... no, not questions... hints... teasing glimpses... the shadows of puzzles mapped onto the future... she shook her head – then continued her move into the TARDIS. The Doctor was waiting with answers to questions she had not yet even learned to ask.

'And I thought babies came with storks,' she giggled with a last look back at the tumultuous sky, and beyond, to the worlds even now being rebuilt by people who had found – and lost – the god within themselves.

As she had lost the god within herself?

As the blue wooden doors closed behind her, she glanced at the Doctor and grinned. 'Come on, Doctor, cheer up. I'll make you some breakfast. How about a little ham and eggs? I hear the green ones are very nice.'

She laughed – too loud and too long

He didn't join in.

Later, she placed the tip of her finger against the hot grill, suffering the pain gladly because it was the sign that would tell her about the future. The future and her place in it.

She waited for the wound to heal.

Epilogue

Ex-navy Captain Ruthelle Bellis stared out at the landscape of Farnham's World. Above her, four crescents shone – new worlds blanketed by the night, a sky rippling with sheets of light. A summer storm to rank in history, its birth had changed the face of a solar system for ever.

As her life had changed.

Changed with the loss of her son, her grandson.

Both gone, swept away by the storm.

But people change. People adapt. They grow. And so she had come here. A new life. A new future.

And regrets?

Only one. One she could do nothing about now, or ever again. Something precious lost, never to be found.

Something she would have to leave behind if she was to move on.

Ruthelle Bellis lifted the six-month-old orphan she had come here to adopt. It was a strong child, born of a strong world. It would need a strong parent. A good start in life. A kick in the right direction.

It had been a long time. Her body would remember.

Goodbyes over, she turned to walk back across the fields, back past the hill-sized machines already imposing human will upon intractable rock, back to First Town. Back to her new home and her new life.

She almost bumped into a strange man wearing a strange look and a frock coat. His hair was as wild as his eyes – wild but somehow gentle.

'Do I know you?'

'I saved your life. Twice, I believe. I thought you'd be needing this.'

He held something out to her. Hefting the child into one arm, she took the object from him. It was a small sliver of paper, grimy, crumpled. A photograph. Her son and grandson.

Her last regret, now at last made whole.

'How did you know?'

His voice was quiet. 'Believe me, I know what it's like to lose someone you love.'

She looked up through tears of memory but the strange man was gone. Something made her glance upward then, searching for the triple crescents of the new planets, the new planets and their single moon.

They were gone too.

Even stars die.

They may grow old, they may seem inconceivable when held against the flickering candle of our own existence, yet they too have lives that are shaped by the same universe, the same immutable laws as are our own lives.

In the measure of Deep Time the brief moment of existence of all the stars in the universe is as the moment a butterfly lives compared with all the summers that will ever be. For the red giant, galactic summer is over and winter is approaching for a second time. Its hydrogen fuel long since exhausted, this old, mad sun has consumed its inner worlds and barely noticed their absence. Burning helium now as a lingering precursor to death, the red giant prepares to shrug off its outer mantle of remaining hydrogen and take its remaining family of planets with it into oblivion.

Within the star, a schism: its core shrinking and growing ever hotter even as its outer layers expand and cool. Soon now will come the moment of death, of explosion – the surviving solar matter burning in a tiny incandescent lump at the heart of a nebula composed of the tattered shreds of its own corpse.

Yet from death comes life. A truth unchanging while there is yet energy in the universe.

While the red giant continues slowly to die, life on its many worlds continues to grow and evolve.

It is a process observed fleetingly by four planet-sized masses as their divergent orbits carry them beyond a solar system now flourishing with the new life they have inadvertently made possible.

ABOUT THE AUTHOR

Matt Forbeck has worked full-time in the adventure game industry for over 15 years. He has designed collectible card games, roleplaying games, miniatures games, and board games, and has written short fiction, comic books, and novels. His previous novels include the critically acclaimed *Secret of the Spiritkeeper* for Wizards of the Coast. *Dead Ball* is his second novel for the Black Library, with the first being *Blood Bowl*.

The Chain: A particular favourite of blitzers everywhere. Players position themselves at different stages upfield. The ball is then quickly passed from player to player in a series of short passes until the blitzer on the end of the chain can wave to the crowd and gallop into the end zone. A broken link in the chain can balls this up (excuse the pun), giving the opposing team an opportunity to intercept the ball.

The Kill-em-all!: Favoured by dwarf teams and those that lack a certain finesse. It works on the principle that if there isn't anyone left in the opposing team, then who's going to stop you from scoring? The receiving team simply hides the ball in its half and proceeds to maul, break and kill the opposition. Chaos teams are particularly good at this. When there is less than a third of the opposing team left, the ball will slowly make its way upfield. The downside is that some teams can get so engrossed in the maiming they simply run out of time to score. Nevertheless it's a fan favourite and is here to stay.